Freedom's Promise
Task Force 125, Book #3

Lisa Pietsch

Table of Contents

Copyright

Published by Defiance Press & Publishing, LLC

Bulk orders of this book may be obtained by contacting Defiance Press & Publishing, LLC. www.defiancepress.com.

Defiance Press & Publishing, LLC

281-581-9300

info@defiancepress.com

Task Force 125 Series

One

Vince Hennessee woke with a start and gasped to find himself sitting in a heavy wooden chair, unable to move. He fought the urge to panic and took a deep breath to calm himself. He tried to kick his feet but they wouldn't budge. Rolling his shoulders, he tugged at the bindings on his wrists.

Duct tape?

He squinted through the dark and made out a few furnishings with the small bit of available natural light coming from the windows. Blinking hard, he wondered what they'd drugged him with. Fighting to focus and remember what happened, he could not will the mental fog away.

Where am I, and how the hell did I get here?

Vince squeezed his eyes shut and opened them again, trying to remember what had happened. Images of being abducted at the airport in Italy flitted through his mind. He'd been on his way to Moscow to meet with Mark Davidson to track down Nikolai.

Somebody hit me, drugged me, and brought me here. But where is here?

Vince knew he had to stay calm, assess the situation, and not do anything foolish. His years as a Recon Marine, seeing more than his share of action in world hot spots, had taught him to remain calm above all else.

His focus was clearer now that the effects of the drug were wearing off and more light shone through the windows.

Sunrise somewhere.

He scanned the room to see mother-of-pearl and gold inlaid on the sideboard, a white marble floor, dark Persian rugs, and Byzantine style windows.

The hairs on the back of his neck bristled as somewhere outside and far off a Muezzin began the Muslim call to prayer. He'd always found the chanting at prayer times moving, but today it was just eerie.

I'm in the Middle East again, but where?

Vince remembered the last time he'd been held hostage in the Middle East. He quickly locked the memory in the back of his mind and forced himself to focus on the present.

Breathe steady. Stay calm. Look for an escape.

The latch clicked on a door somewhere behind him. Every muscle tensed involuntarily. He breathed deeply to calm his nerves.

A drop of sweat raced from his right temple to his jaw.

Stay calm.

Two

Sarah Stevens examined the toe of her black, leather Prada slingback and gasped. A huge scuff glared at her. She sighed with relief as she wiped the spot with a tissue and restored the shoe to its original glory. The overstuffed back seat of the Rolls Royce Silver Seraph limousine embraced her as she leaned back and glanced out the window.

"Not a bad way to get from point A to point B, huh?"

She turned to smile at Will Adams. With their team leader, her boyfriend, Vince Hennessee missing in action, Will was in charge now.

Will dressed and carried himself like a man who had the world at his fingertips, because he did. Will had once been a medic in the Navy, but Sarah suspected there was much more to that story. Though he began his career as a Corpsman, Sarah expected he'd done a bit more than first aid to make the rank of Master Chief before he left the service for a position on Task Force 125. He was the team's second in command, capable of finding any supplies they needed on a moment's notice. With Vince missing, the entire team fell in line behind him without question. He'd also worked undercover with Vince for years as an arms dealer.

Sarah took comfort in Will's leadership and grasped the glimmer of hope she saw in his baby blue eyes. They would find and recover Vince.

Will nodded slightly toward the front of the limousine. "There it is, the Burj al Arab, Dubai's crown jewel."

Sarah's jaw dropped. She gawked at the glorious structure rising majestically over the water ahead of them as they drove along the causeway.

She remembered just over a year ago when she was an overweight Air Force cop with no future. She gave thanks that her commander had realized her potential and referred her to what she thought was a fat camp. That weight loss program turned out to be one of the C.I.A.'s training farms for paramilitary operatives. Little did she know at the time that losing her police job, her cheating boyfriend, and seventy-five pounds would make it possible for her to ride in Rolls Royce limos wearing Prada and Versace, not to mention the pearls around her neck that cost more than her car. She fingered them lovingly and recalled with a smile the day Vince had given her the necklace.

As though he'd read her mind, Will smiled his winning smile. "You've come a long way, baby."

They pulled up at the curb in front of the seven star hotel, and Sarah sighed. "Yes, I have."

Jason hopped out of the front passenger seat and opened Sarah's door for her. "Welcome to Oz." He beamed with his trademark Cheshire cat grin. Anyone who saw Jason would think he was happy to be staying at the glorious Burj al Arab, but Sarah knew better.

Jason Williams, the former Green Beret and the team's weapons specialist, was always spoiling for a fight, and he knew he was going to have a big one when they took Vince back. Since she'd joined the team, Sarah and Jason had become great friends. He was a mixed martial arts master and damn impressive in a fight. For months now, he'd been teaching Sarah how to fight and win in just about any situation. He'd also been kind enough to squire her around Las Vegas to all his favorite watering holes.

A tall handsome Arab man dressed in a silk Armani suit greeted Sarah, Jason, and Will at the curb as they stepped out of the Rolls Royce. They were all dressed to the nines, Armani being the suit of the day for Jason and Will, too. The greeter smiled slightly. "Mr. Adamson, welcome to the Burj al Arab. Your suite is ready. If you will follow me." He turned and escorted them into the lobby.

Adamson was one of Will's aliases. What they were doing here was not sanctioned by the C.I.A. If they were lucky, the Agency would never find out about their plan to recapture their kidnapped leader, who was being held somewhere in the Middle East. They were all using aliases on this trip. Sarah's was Elisabetta Scuro, an Italian alias in honor of the recently deceased Angelo Scuro who not only died on their last mission but left Sarah his vast estate in Italy.

The hotel's service was immediate and excellent, but Sarah couldn't help being annoyed at the time that was passing, precious seconds that meant the difference between life and death for Vince. The flight to Dubai had provided her with far too much time to think about what his captors might be doing to him. She pushed the dark thoughts of Vince being

6

tortured and beaten from her mind and tried to stay focused on the task at hand.

They were here to meet with Mark Davidson, an agent none of them had met, who had information on where Vince was being held. Davidson's contacts had found out about Vince's kidnapping, and he'd known to contact Will at Sarah's estate in Italy. Sarah ran through the list of things they'd need to do before they could even begin planning an attack to get Vince back. After they checked in to their suite at the hotel, they'd make contact with Davidson, who was working under an official cover in the U.S. State Department in Saudi Arabia. Then they'd wait for their other teammates, Brian Allen and Chris Wilson to arrive in Dubai. All of this meant more passing time.

Worries vanished from Sarah's mind as she gasped at the overwhelming opulence of the Burj al Arab. Massive golden columns encircled the lobby and reached toward the sweeping arches above. The mesmerizing mosaic on the floor in deep blue, red and gold nearly stopped her in her tracks. Sarah looked at Jason wide eyed.

Jason grinned and paused with Sarah while Will continued toward the elevator with their host. "Shock and awe, eh, sweetcheeks? This place makes Vegas look like a two bit whore."

She grinned at Jason. "Speaking of whores, did I tell you how fine you look in that suit?"

He smoothed the front of his jacket with his right hand and extended his left arm for her. "I guess you won't mind being seen with me then?"

"Not at all, handsome." She looped her right arm through his, and they picked up their pace to meet Will and their host at the elevator. Her Prada shoes tapped along the ornate marble floor as she took in the rich colors and happy international chatter coming from vacationers and businesspeople.

Their host escorted them into a private elevator, and they rode to the twenty-fifth floor of the all suite hotel. Sarah held the rail tightly as they whisked fifty stories skyward.

Sarah tried to remain calm as she wondered where Vince might be and took a long, deep breath as their host opened the door to their two-story suite. On the other side of the glistening marble entryway rose a marble and gold staircase covered with leopard print carpeting. She was overwhelmed, instantly enveloped in luxury while her mind swam in thoughts of the horrible things that could be happening to Vince. Sarah gripped Jason's arm tightly to keep the only grasp on reality she had.

He leaned close and smiled as he whispered to her. "Any other time I'd love your manicured nails digging into my skin, but the blood you draw today will ruin my Armani."

Jason's teasing was all Sarah needed to shock her back to reality. This over-the-top extravagance was her life now. Angelo had left her an enormous estate in Italy and more money than she'd ever dreamed of having. Once Vince was free, they'd leave the Agency and start enjoying it together.

Better start getting used to it now.

She retracted her claws and gave Jason an apologetic pout as she mouthed the words, "I'm sorry."

Three

Nikolai breezed into the room smelling of a hot shower and expensive aftershave. "Good morning, Vince. I thought you might sleep all day."

Obviously, you misjudged the amount of sedative you shot me up with.

Nikolai walked behind Vince and cut his wrists free.

Vince pulled the duct tape off his wrists and a good bit of hair with it, leaving them red and raw. He stretched his arms over his head and was now more than aware of his own body odor and the filthy condition of his T-shirt and jeans. He surmised wherever they'd kept him while they transported him from Italy to—*wherever this is*—it wasn't clean and it most definitely hadn't been cool.

He tried to act calm. "Nikolai. I've been looking for you. Thanks for sparing me the hassle of…well, consciousness while I did it." He examined the room slowly, careful to take in as many details as possible. "Nice place. Is it yours?"

Vince guessed by the light now coming through the windows that it was midmorning. He faced an antique wooden desk. To his left on the eastern wall was a large stained glass window of mostly blue panes that received direct sunlight at sunrise. The floor was covered with oriental-style rugs that complimented the light cream stucco walls.

This large room must have originally been intended as a prayer room.

"Thank you. It is one of many." Nikolai pulled up a heavy, elaborately carved, wooden chair and sat facing Vince. He pulled out a pack of Marlboro Reds and lit one. He offered the cigarette to Vince. "It might help that metallic taste you have in your mouth."

"Thanks. That's very considerate of you." Vince took the cigarette.

Nikolai grinned. "I would apologize for drugging you but it made transportation so much easier." He lit a cigarette for himself, then sat back in his chair and took a long drag. He blew the smoke out slowly as he eyed Vince. "So tell me about Sarah Stevens." He waited.

The prickle of every little hair standing on end, from his shoulder blades to his head, reminded Vince to check his emotions.

Keep cool, man. He doesn't know anything.

Vince grinned. "What? No tour of the house? No 'let's have a drink and chat?'"

Nikolai frowned. He didn't seem interested in any of Vince's small talk. His eyes narrowed, and he huffed smoke from his nose. He wanted information, and it appeared he wanted it yesterday.

Okay, time to tap dance.

"Sarah Stevens, huh?" Vince took a thoughtful puff of his cigarette and browsed the room for a moment. "Not much to tell. She's got a great ass, I know that. I think she's a student at the University in Las Vegas. She's big on the party circuit. That's about all I know."

Nikolai spat the word from his mouth. "Bullshit."

Four

Just as their host left the suite, Will's phone chirped from the breast pocket of his silk suit. He slipped it out quickly and looked at the caller I.D.

Sarah stared at him, anxious for any word about Vince. "Who is it?"

Will smiled and spoke softly. "It's Chris."

She sighed and set her Louis Vuitton handbag on the leopard print sofa and continued to pace nervously.

"Hey, Chris. Where are you?" He walked over to the silver platter laden with fruit and plucked a strawberry from the top. "Okay. It's on time? Good. Call me when you land." He slipped his Blackberry back into his jacket pocket and the strawberry into his mouth.

"Where are they, Will?"

"They're in London. They got a nonstop flight so they'll be here tonight."

Sarah rolled her head from left to right to work out a kink in her neck. "Good."

Will picked an apple from the fruit tray and took a bite. "Take a load off and have some fruit." He gestured with the apple. "This is amazing."

"No thanks." Sarah paced the large traditional Arab receiving room lined with plush sofas. She listened to the tap-tap-tap of her shoes on the marble and willed Chris and Brian's flight to travel at the speed of light. She plucked her gold cigarette case from her handbag and slipped a cigarette out, then tapped the filter end repeatedly against the gold trinket just to keep her hands busy. "Jesus, Will. Nikolai could be beating the shit out of Vince right now."

Will grabbed her by the arm and stopped her pacing. He spoke slowly. "Sarah, it's an eight-hour flight. I know you're upset but you're going to have to get a grip and keep your head in the game, otherwise you're no good to us or to Vince. We're going into this with a skeleton crew as it is. We need all hands on this."

Jason bounced into the room with a smile from ear to ear. "You gotta check out the can in this joint." He stopped when he saw the look on Will's face. "What's going on?"

Will tipped his head toward Sarah and threw back an imaginary shot, giving Jason the universal signal for "Get that woman a couple of drinks" and Jason nodded. "I'm gonna go make some phone calls. Why don't you guys order some room service?"

Jason checked the bar in the corner of the room and picked up the house phone. "Yeah, can we get a pitcher of Margaritas brought up?" There was a pause. "No, we don't need a bartender, thank you." He bobbed his head. "Yeah, that'll be perfect. Thank you."

Jason hung up the phone and walked over to Sarah, who was standing with her arms across her chest, looking out to sea. He wrapped his arms around her in a reassuring hug. "Vince knows how to survive, Sarah. He's gonna be just fine."

Sarah slumped, leaned back onto Jason's chest, and sighed.

"I don't know how to do this, and I hate it."

"Sarah, he's a Marine. He's Force Recon. He spent his entire military career behind enemy lines. He's done this before."

"I know, but I haven't."

The butler returned. Sarah wondered how many black morning coats and white gloves a Burj al Arab butler went through in a week. He set a silver platter containing a crystal pitcher of mixed margaritas, several glasses, and an ice bucket on the bar. He nodded to Jason. "Shall I serve, sir?"

Jason smiled and slid a couple twenty dirham notes into his hand. "Thank you. We'll serve. That'll be all."

The butler bowed slightly and slipped away as quickly and as quietly as he'd come in.

Jason poured a drink for Sarah and one for himself. "Come on, girl. Let's have a drink and enjoy this view."

Sarah gazed out over the Palm islands and wondered where in the real world Vince was. Her heart ached to think he might be in pain while she and the rest of the team were living in the lap of luxury. "I don't want a drink. I want to be clear." Sarah pressed her right hand to her left shoulder and rolled the shoulder slowly with a grimace.

"All right, talk to Papa. How's that gunshot wound healing? You want something for the pain?"

12

"Nah, it's just a little stiff from the travel. A little yoga and I'll be good as new. Don't you feel guilty, Jase? Here we are in the lap of luxury and who knows where Vince is or what he's going through?"

"Guilt isn't a productive emotion. When you stay in this sort of business long enough, you learn to shut it off." He handed Sarah the Margarita. "Nikolai speaks the international language of money. He wants something only Vince can give him, probably you, and that means he'll keep Vince alive and happy. Trust me, living with his ex-wife was more threatening than a few days with the Russian will be."

Sarah remembered her own experience with Vince's ex-wife, commonly referred to by her teammates as "The Hell Bitch." She nodded slightly. "You could be right."

"It's been known to happen." Jason smiled like a Cheshire cat. "Sarah, we can't do a damned thing until Brian and Chris get here so you've got a full eight hours to get foggy and clear up again." His voice dropped an octave and seemed more commanding than friendly. "Sit down and have a frigging drink, woman."

Sarah sighed and followed orders. Jason rarely gave them, but, when he did, she knew it was in her best interest to pay attention. "Okay." She parked herself on the leopard print sofa and sipped the cold, tart beverage.

"You know what I love about the Middle East?"

Sarah watched Jason as he took a seat beside her and swallowed half his drink in one gulp. "The dry heat?"

He glared at her. "Hell no. It's humid most places except the Rub' al Kali. What I love is the fact that smoking is still accepted and non-smoking hotel rooms are the exception." He slipped two cigarettes out of his pack and lit them at the same time, handing her one of them.

She recalled the cigarette she'd taken from her case earlier and looked into her hand to see the tragic remains in her sweaty palm.

Some secret agent I am. Can't even handle a little job-related stress.

Jason chortled as he wiped the tobacco mess from her hand into his. "Now what the hell did that cigarette ever do to you to be treated like that?" He dusted the tobacco and paper into a nearby potted plant.

Sarah took a drink of her margarita and a drag from the new cigarette and smiled weakly at Jason. "I'm a mess, aren't I?"

He nodded. "You're new to this. You didn't train to be on the waiting end. You trained to be *Action Girl*. You're all tensed and ready for a fight but, it isn't going to happen today and probably won't even happen tomorrow."

Sarah set her drink on the table in front of her, leaned back, and closed her eyes. She wished this were all a dream and she'd wake up in Italy to Vince bringing her coffee in bed. A low groan escaped her lips.

"Sarah, you trust me, right?" He picked up her glass and nodded for her to drink more.

"Of course, I do, Jason." She took a sip of her drink while she listened.

"I'm gonna tell you a little something, and I hope you'll pay attention."

She turned to face him. "Okay, shoot."

"That adrenaline high you're on isn't going to last. It's a short-term drug and when it runs out, you're gonna crash. You'll crash hard just like you did after we got back from that first mission against Hassan. Remember all the adrenaline you rode to get yourself and Vince off that yacht when Hassan found out who you were? And do you remember how long you slept afterwards?"

Sarah recalled their first mission. Hassan was a major moneyman for Al Qaeda, and he had been hot for her. She'd had a great cover as his girlfriend, and Vince as an arms dealer until Hassan figured out that Vince wasn't just an arms dealer. She managed to save Vince from execution on Hassan's yacht, but she blew her cover in the process. Hassan tried to use her as leverage against Vince but ended up shooting Vince instead. Sarah had just enough time to stab Hassan in the heart, grab Vince, and jump off the yacht before it exploded. She never would have been able to lift a big, muscular guy like Vince without the assistance of adrenaline, and lots of it. "Oh, yeah. I slept for two and a half days. I woke up hungry as a bear."

Jason took a last, hard drag and stubbed his cigarette out in the crystal ashtray. "That adrenaline sucks every bit of energy out of you. You need to conserve that energy until we know what we're up against. Save it. Relax, have a few drinks, and then get some rest so you're fresh when Chris and Brian get here." He drank the last of his margarita and set the glass on the table in front of the sofa. "Then we can take stock and get this operation going."

She nodded and took a long drink, collecting what thoughts she could. "Jason, how can you be so calm? We declared war on Nikolai's organization when we smoked his top arms dealer. Now he's kidnapped Vince and God only knows what he'll do to him to get back at us. Every minute we waste could be Vince's last."

Jason chuckled and shook his head. "It doesn't work that way, girl. This sort of thing is a dance. Vince has been doing what he does for a long time. Force Recon guys train to operate behind enemy lines. They prepare for capture. It's a whole different world from what you've done, but he knows all the moves. He's a master at tricks and mind games." Jason leaned back into the sofa and grinned wide. "Trust me, Vince is king of the mind fuck. If Nikolai knows anything about Vince, or us, then he knows he's sitting on a gold mine of intelligence. He'll keep Vince healthy and alive unless Vince does something stupid." Jason lit a fresh cigarette. "And Vince is one guy who never does anything stupid."

~~~

Will walked into the sitting room and found Jason with his feet on the plush sofa and a satisfied grin on his face.

"Where's Sarah?"

Jason took a drag of his cigarette, blew a smoke ring, and pointed to the empty pitcher on a silver platter nearby. "Adrenaline crash plus tequila makes for a sleepy Sarah."

Will shook his head. "I gotta hand it to you brother, for a guy who doesn't know jack about women, you handle that particular woman pretty well."

"What can I say?" Jason shrugged. "It's a gift. Besides, she thinks more like a guy than a woman. Where did you get on the phone calls?"

Will sat on the sofa and took his first look at the view they had from high above the ocean. "My God, this place is spectacular."

"It's fucking awesome. I've never seen anything like it."

Will looked over at Jason who was waiting for news on Will's calls. "You know the work Vince and I did allowed us to put a few nest eggs away, right?"

"Yeah." Jason knew Vince and Will had skimmed a little off the top for *insurance* when they negotiated arms deals for the U.S. government. It was the only way agents could cover their asses when working for a bunch of bureaucrats who might turn around and screw them without a moment's hesitation, just like Vince was being screwed right now. That *insurance* was money they needed to fall back on now because the Agency had disavowed any association with Vince and refused to send in a rescue team when he'd been kidnapped. The C.I.A. didn't give a damn that it was their bad intel that left an opening for Nikolai Federov, the man they should have been after in their last mission, to get away.

Will continued speaking in generalities just in case their stealthy butler happened to walk in on their conversation. Their plan was to act like real estate investors while in the hotel.

"Well, I called my banker here in Dubai, and we have a practically unlimited budget for any purchases we choose to make."

Jason smiled wide. "Excellent."

"I also made a call to a buddy of mine in Las Vegas. Nikolai's mother lives there, and I thought she might help negotiations."

Jason leaned forward. "Yeah? What happened?"

"Official word at the University is she's taken a leave of absence for a family emergency back in Russia."

"Family emergency. You bet your babka it's an emergency. There's no chance of getting to her there. I've got to hand it to that guy, he knows how to cover his bases."

"Hey, it was worth a shot." Will yawned and loosened his tie. "I'm going to catch a nap before the guys get here. What room did Sarah take?"

"She took one of the kings upstairs. I'll just nap down here if you want the other king bed and then Brian and Chris can have the twins."

Will smiled and slapped Jason on the shoulder. "You saved the day with Sarah and now you're taking one for the team by sleeping on a plush sofa overlooking the Arabian Gulf. You're a noble man."

"Yeah, it's all good. Too much luxury makes me nervous. Sleeping on one of those ultra pillow-top beds might just throw me into convulsions."

Will chuckled and shook his head. "You'd still be more comfortable in a foxhole or a bird's nest, wouldn't you?"

Jason stretched out on the sofa and laced his fingers together behind his neck. "You've got that right."

Five

"Lucy, I'm home!"

Sarah had never been so happy to hear Brian's voice. She scrambled out of her room and to the top of the golden staircase to see Brian Allen and Chris Wilson, looking fresh as daisies in designer suits, standing in the elegant marble entryway. She leaned on the railing and smiled down at them.

Brian and Chris standing side by side covered just about every woman's fantasy.

Brian stood well over six feet, had a well-muscled physique and not one ounce of body fat. His dark brown hair and eyes and tanned, chiseled features made him look about as exotic as you can get for a guy who grew up in Texas. After fifteen years as a Navy SEAL, Brian had been recruited to the C.I.A.'s Special Activities Division for his combat experience and knowledge of all things explosive. Brian's special gift was being able to pick up the hottest woman in any room, love her, leave her, and still remain friends.

Sarah responded in kind. "That's good 'cuz someone's got some 'splainin' to do."

Chris grinned up at her. He stood just short of six feet and, on casual days, looked the part of a surfer. Dressed in Armani, he was a blond-haired, blue-eyed hunk of hotness. He could sweet talk a woman in seven languages other than English while he did a background check so comprehensive he'd know how many times a day her bowels moved.

Whenever Sarah went undercover, Chris' was the voice in her miniscule earpiece, keeping in constant contact with her, twenty-four seven. Consequently, he also knew the details of her sex life and bowels, something that took Sarah a little getting used to, but Chris, the team's communications expert, was nothing if not discreet.

Brian looked up at Sarah. "Well, hey, darlin'." His face dropped. "You look like shit."

She let the comment roll off her back. If Brian said it, it was probably true. He never minced words. "I thought you guys would never get here." Sarah walked down the stairs and greeted them both with hugs.

Chris held her at arm's length and looked her over. "How are you doing? How's the shoulder? Still much pain?"

"I'm okay." She demonstrated by rolling her shoulder with only a hint of pain. "I'm glad to be out of the sling. Accessorizing an outfit while wearing a sling is like putting paint on shit. It still looks like shit." She turned to Brian. "I'm ready to kick somebody's ass though."

Brian wrapped his arm around Sarah's waist and they walked into the sitting room. "Well, now you know how we feel when we're waiting to pull you out of an operation. I don't know what you're getting so riled up about. This ain't nothin' but another mission, darlin'."

Chris nodded in agreement as he scanned the area for electronic listening devices. The Burj al Arab was well known for its discretion and having bugs in the suites would be a disaster for business. But Chris was the best at what he did and nobody on the team questioned his desire to ensure operational security.

Sarah stopped, looked at Brian, and suddenly saw things from their point of view. "How do you do it?"

Brian wrinkled his brow. "Do what?"

"Act like it's no big thing and stay so cool."

"Well, first of all, we're all very cool to begin with." He nodded a hello to Will who strolled into the room with his signature smile and sparkling blue eyes. "We've all had years of operational experience so, no matter what happens, we've probably seen worse. Each of us has a different way of keeping a cap on the stress. I lift a few more weights, Will cooks a lot and writes lists," Will rolled his eyes as he looked down at the legal pad in his hand, "Jason smokes like a chimney and cleans his guns, Vince plans the attack and several hundred contingency plans, and Chris reads thrillers and hacks into satellites."

Chris shrugged. "In all fairness, Sarah doesn't spend all her time talking when she's undercover. I can't just listen to dead air all the time."

Brian stood a good eight inches over Sarah and looked down at her. "Let me guess, you've been having some trouble with the waiting?"

Sarah frowned, disappointed in her inability to just roll with the situation like the rest of them seemed to do. "Yeah, a little."

"All right." Brian smiled at her with a combination of pity and simple indulgence. He held her hands firmly so she couldn't continue fidgeting. "How 'bout you fix us some drinks while we clean up and then we'll talk about this? We can't have our best girl gettin' all nervous on us, can we?"

Sarah walked into the main salon while Brian and Chris climbed the stairs to the bedrooms. She caught a glimpse of herself in one of the gold framed mirrors and realized Brian hadn't been kidding. She ran her fingers through her hair and tried to look a little less frazzled. She poured two glasses of Scotch for Brian and Chris and paced the floor in front of the massive, wall-sized window overlooking the Arabian Gulf.

Chris strolled into the room and gave Sarah a hug. "No offense, doll, but you've looked better. I know you've been through a lot but remember your cover. You're a real estate investor. You're loaded and the real estate market here has gone bust. You're about to purchase crown jewels at bargain-basement prices. This is a shopper's dream. You should look a little more, uh, happy."

Sarah's cheeks warmed with embarrassment. She took a step back and blinked hard as she considered Chris' words. "You're right. I need to bring my A-game and I'm looking C-minus at best."

Chris shrugged. "I didn't say that, but now that you mention it, a C-minus is generous."

Brian's voice boomed as he skipped down the stairs two at a time. "You got that right, darlin!" He held his arms out. "What's next? You gonna come crawlin down here in sweats and eating pints of ice cream?"

Sarah winced at the thought.

Brian wrapped an arm around her waist and kissed her on the cheek. "Where's that drink you promised me?"

Sarah handed them their Scotch as Jason strolled into the room and pointed to the amber liquid. "Can I have one of those?"

Sarah nodded, happy to have something to do, even if it was tending bar. "Just remember to tip your waitress."

Brian greeted Jason with their usual half hug. "Great timing, man. We're just about to have a chat with Sarah about how the other half, meaning us, lives."

Jason rubbed the back of his muscled neck with his free hand. "Good." He took the crystal glass Sarah offered. "I tried to explain that earlier but she was a little jetlagged. I don't think she absorbed it all."

Brian lounged in one of the overstuffed chairs and casually crossed his left ankle over his right knee. He took a sip and savored it, closing his eyes and pausing for a moment before swallowing. "Mm...good stuff. God forbid you should get top shelf liquor on a commercial flight nowadays. Private jets have ruined me for all other means of travel."

In the interest of speed and anonymity, Chris and Brian had booked commercial flights instead of the usual private jet provided by the C.I.A. Sarah chided herself for fretting about how long they took to arrive when she considered that they had been flying coach or stuck in airports for the past twenty-four hours.

Brian turned his brown eyes to Sarah. He looked kindly on her as he spoke. "Okay, you haven't worked this end of a deal before so it's only natural for you to feel a little out of your element. You're usually sunning on a yacht or at a mansion somewhere while we do all the waiting, sweating and background work."

Sarah knew he was right and couldn't argue. She gave a weak smile in acknowledgement as Brian continued.

"Working this side of an operation requires patience. There's a lot you can learn on this end, but you need to stay on your toes and out of your insecurities so you can observe everything we do with a clear head. We need you working with us here. If you're tense and stressed, you won't be any good to us and you'll just slow us down. If that's the case, we might as well send you back now. You don't want to put us in that position, do you?"

Hard words but the professional in her knew he was right.

Six

Vince opened his eyes and blinked several times.

What the hell are they using to knock me out?

The room was pitch black, cool, and dry. No sounds from the outside. He sat up. There was a cot under him.

No mattress, no blanket. Thanks for nothing.

He ran his hand over the hair that had grown out on his usually shaved head. "I've got to stop waking up hung over in strange places." The sound of his own voice was something of a comfort in captivity.

He reached out to feel around him.

Concrete floor. Concrete wall.

He stood and reached toward the ceiling. It was only a few inches taller than he was.

At least I can stand and stretch my legs.

He felt his way around the perimeter of the room, pacing off the length and width.

Six feet wide and eight feet long. All concrete. Must be a storage room.

When he reached the door, he traced it with his fingertips.

No hinges. No doorknob. Opens from the outside.

He kicked the door a few times to test it for weakness.

Solid wood. I won't be able to break through it.

He swallowed hard and choked back his fear of being buried alive, something he'd carried with him since a cave-in during an operation in Afghanistan

A valid concern and an easy option, but Nikolai is too smart to kill me—yet.

He followed the walls again, this time systematically feeling along every inch for cracks, openings or any sign of weakness.

Nothing.

He crawled on his hands and knees to feel every inch of the floor.

Great. They left me a ceramic pot under the cot. Nice. Not much of a weapon but it could work. If it's light out there when they open the door,

I'll be blind for a few seconds after they open it. That gives them enough time to get the advantage.

Vince heard footsteps. He cocked his head toward the sound, straining to hear.

Two men. Concrete floor.

A set of keys jingled and one key clicked into the lock.

A voice warned him from the other side of the door. "Don't try anything stupid, mate. I've been paid so I'm not averse to shooting you now." Vince recognized the voice of the Australian who had snatched him at the airport.

He sat on the cot and waited.

Seven

Sarah sat back, took a sip of the Cabernet Sauvignon served with dinner and looked around the table at Will, Jason, Brian, and Chris—four of the most intelligent, talented, and interesting men she'd ever met. Four men she loved more than family. Each of them was a skilled operative, and each had his own reasons for putting his CIA career on the line for Vince.

She shook her head as she realized the immense gravity of the situation. That's exactly what they were all doing—jeopardizing their careers to rescue Vince from eventual but certain death. If they were picked up by local police or intelligence personnel, their identities would be flagged by the Agency within hours, and they'd be locked up for as long as the local authorities wanted to keep them. They had flown in under the radar, on aliases with forged passports, and they were using offshore funds from numbered accounts. They'd all be sent to jail for the rest of their natural lives if the Agency got wind of what they were up to.

In spite of all that, this was about honor. The only code that mattered to anyone who had ever served in any military branch. You never leave a brother to die. You fight. You kill. You may even die trying to save him, but it is an honorable way to go.

After the butler finished serving the salad course, Will dismissed him. "Thank you. We'll do the rest." Will nodded to Brian who stood and locked the service door after he watched the butler disappear down the corridor.

Will set his utensils on his dinner plate and took a drink of wine before continuing. "We have a helicopter arriving to pick us up in two hours. It'll take us directly to the island and drop us off. The pilot is Leo, a Navy buddy of mine, so it should be comfortable transport, and he knows to keep it on the down low. Once he drops us off, we'll have access to everything we'll need, including several modes of transportation, which Brian will handle.

Brian grinned. "Excellent."

"There is a fully equipped office for Chris and some of Jason's favorite things to keep him busy."

Jason bobbed his head and replied in the tune of an old C&C Music Factory song. "Things that make you go *boom*."

Will flashed him a look that said "stop." "There will also be some literature for all of us to examine. From there, we'll get in touch with our broker in Saudi Arabia."

Sarah understood what he meant to say, but didn't for fear of nosy staff. They'd have safe transport to a secure facility where they would have access to vehicles, arms, state-of-the-art satellite technology, and secure communication. Their "broker" was Mark Davidson, the only Agency guy willing to help them rescue Vince. Davidson had called Will out of the blue at Sarah's new home in Italy to inform them Vince had been kidnapped.

~~~

The team waited in the lounge on the roof of the Burj al Arab, drinking overpriced bottled water in blue designer bottles. The porter waited outside on the helipad with their luggage on a brass rolling cart.

The helicopter landed at exactly eleven p.m. according to the new Chopard watch Sarah'd bought from a shop in the lobby. The chopper touched down without the slightest rocking on the big painted "H." Will stood and straightened his silk suit jacket, closing the buttons he'd loosened when he sat. He strolled onto the helipad just outside the lounge and up to the pilot's door, which opened as he reached it. Sarah watched through the lounge window to see Will's pilot friend, Leo, was a bear of a man, complete with a Grizzly Adams beard. He wore blue jeans and a black T-shirt, a look that inspired dismay in the porter's face. Sarah chuckled. She imagined nobody ever landed at the Burj al Arab wearing anything so casual. Leo stepped out of the chopper and gave Will a half handshake, half man-hug. They exchanged words and nods.

Will waved them outside as the pilot showed the porter where to stow their luggage.

Sarah took a moment to admire Brian, Chris and Jason all suited up, starched, and lightly bearded with fresh haircuts. They really did look the part of wealthy investors.

Wealthy investors who can kick ass.

Sarah checked her reflection in the glass. She looked her part, too, from her Prada pumps to her midnight blue Versace dress accessorized with the twenty thousand dollar pearl necklace Vince had given her.

Sarah took the hand Will offered as she stepped up into the helicopter. She nestled into one of the ultra plush, velour seats in the back. Jason sat in the one next to her.

Chris and Will sat in the middle row while Brian sat in the copilot seat. After liftoff, Brian and Leo talked the whole flight to the island.

Sarah couldn't make out what was said, but she gathered most of it was pilot talk and coordinate speak.

They flew mostly low and over the Gulf. It was somewhat disconcerting to be flying so close to the water at night but Sarah trusted Will's judgment in choosing the pilot. Everything Will did was first class, and she had no reason to believe this was any different.

She gazed out over the inky blackness, excited to finally know the rescue mission was in motion.

Hold on, Vince.

Eight

Less than a half hour after they left the Burj al Arab, they set down on a dark helipad on what seemed to be a completely uninhabited island. Sarah could make out a few buildings in the faint moonlight but thought it odd there weren't any security lights.

All of the buildings on the island were dark. The place looked deserted and that was probably a good thing. Leo stayed in the chopper while the team disembarked and retrieved their luggage, pulling it clear before waving goodbye to someone they might never see again. They watched the helicopter lift off quickly and buzz away quietly into the night. In a few moments, it was out of sight.

Suddenly, a zillion watts of floodlight shocked Sarah like a deer on a country road. No matter which way she turned, there was blinding light in her eyes.

Will's voice boomed. "Hit the deck!"

Someone tackled Sarah and threw her to the ground.

Adrenaline shot through her veins as she tensed to fight. She heard Jason's voice in her ear, "Be ready."

He had thrown her to the ground and lay over her like any good bodyguard would. He pressed the handle of a Bowie knife into Sarah's palm.

A man's voice cut through the night. "Lie down on your bellies and put your hands behind your backs. You're on my island, so do it now, bitches."

Sarah heard Brian growl. "This ain't right, Will. These were our coordinates."

Will mumbled back to Brian. "I know. This is Vince's island and whoever this squatter is, he's going to have some serious explaining to do."

"Cut the chatter and tell me just what the hell you're doing here!" The stranger's voice had moved.

Will's voice shot out with indignance. "Wait one damned minute. I know that voice! Guinea Man? Is that you, you son of a bitch?"

The man's voice came from another direction this time. Whoever he was he could move like a tactical machine.

"Who's askin'?"

"Will Adams."

The stranger's voice lifted. "Billy boy? Well I'll be damned!"

Some of the lights went out and made seeing a little easier.

Will stood and brushed off his suit. "Get up, guys."

Jason gave Sarah a hand. "Sorry about that tackle."

"That's okay, Jase." She rubbed the sand from her hands before she started brushing it from her dress. If they had been attacked, Jason would have taken a bullet for her and that tackle proved it. "It was quite thoughtful, really."

Sarah took stock of the damage to her clothes as the rest of the team recovered and dusted off their suits.

Will smiled as he greeted a thinly built man in his late thirties wearing old jeans and a white T-shirt. "You son of a bitch. I'd know that down east accent anywhere. I thought you were dead!"

The stranger ran a hand through his shoulder length, dark hair but it flopped back into his eyes in spite of his effort. "Yeah, well the stories of my demise were grossly exaggerated but let's just keep that our secret. Vince is letting me stay here on the sly." He glanced at Chris, Brian, Jason, and Sarah—then did a double-take on Sarah. "Who are these bums?"

"Don't worry. They're cool. Can we cut these lights and talk inside? It's as bright as the sun out here, and we'd rather not draw any more attention while we're here."

"Sure." He tilted his head toward the house. "I take it you're gonna tell me why Vince isn't here with you?"

"Yep." Will picked up his bags and motioned for everyone else to do the same.

The guy Will called Guinea Man pulled a remote from his pocket, pushed a button and all the lights, other than the security lamps went out. Sarah took a moment to adjust to the darkness again. Something on her shoe caught her eye. "Damnit!" The tumble to the tarmac had taken a giant gash out of her Prada.

What the hell is going on here? I'm liking this less every hour.

Sarah and the boys picked up their bags and followed Guinea Man along the concrete path, through a modestly landscaped yard to the house.

He held the front door open as they filed into the large, stucco mansion. He did his best to undress Sarah with his eyes as she walked through. "You always travel with your girlfriend, Billy, or is she for me?"

Will spoke over his shoulder. "That's Vince's girl, Guinea. I'd think twice about making a move on her if I were you. If she doesn't kill you for trying, he will."

Guinea Man followed a little too close behind Sarah for her comfort. "Aw, she couldn't hurt a flea."

Will's voice came across loud and clear. "There are some dead guys who might disagree."

Guinea Man gaped at Sarah. "No shit?"

Sarah glared at him and spun the big knife in her hand at eye level. "Yeah, no shit, dickhead."

Jason lunged between them and grabbed the knife. He tucked it away in a sheath under his jacket and smiled at Guinea Man. "Best not to let her have these when she's pissed off. Vince's ex had to learn that lesson the hard way."

How does Jason read me so well?

Guinea man took a wide-eyed and cautious step back. "Bet you're a real alley cat in the sack."

Sarah took a deep breath as she tried to keep a cap on her rising anger.

"I know you've been out of circulation a while, Guinea, but some of our agents are female now. Show a little respect. Sarah's earned it."

"You gotta be kidding me, Billy."

Sarah really wasn't feeling any love for this guy. The only thing between him and becoming hamburger was Will's goodwill toward him.

"Okay, normally I'd let her fight you because it would be quicker to prove, but she's still recovering from a gunshot wound so I'll give you the tally instead. She took out two pirates who had all of us at gunpoint, cut the throat of a guy who was about to execute Vince, cut the heart out of a guy who shot Vince, took a bullet meant for either me or Vince in our last op and...stop me when you've heard enough."

Guinea Man waved his hand dismissively at Will. "Yeah, yeah. I get it. She's an American badass." He smirked at Sarah and shrugged. "You're still a babe. You want some coffee?"

Sarah looked the guy over. He was old school, and she could respect that. In her years in the Air Force, she'd met very few women who could hold their own. They certainly hadn't made it any easier for her. She nodded. "Yeah, coffee would be a good start."

~~~

They all stood around the island in Vince's gourmet kitchen drinking the coffee Guinea Man had already had brewed.

Chris stirred a spoonful of creamer into his coffee. "Were you expecting somebody or do you always have a pot of coffee on?"

Guinea shrugged. "I like my coffee. Besides, I usually take a walk around the island every few hours and like to take a cup with me. It's always been a peaceful walk until tonight." Guinea Man pulled a travel mug out of an old M-16 ammo pouch hanging from his belt.

Will nodded. "That's Guinea. Don't mess with his coffee or his smokes. You still smoking?"

"Hell yeah. I'm dead already so why quit?"

Sarah sniffed the warm coffee, recognized the aroma, and took a gulp. "This tastes just like Dunkin Donuts coffee."

"Yeah, I get it shipped in by the case. If you're gonna be stranded on a deserted island, you might as well have good coffee, right?"

Sarah and Jason both nodded.

Brian seemed agitated. "All right, I hate to be rude and interrupt the coffee klatch here, but we've got important shit to do and time's a wastin' so let's get down to business and exchange some information."

"Brian is right." Will pointed at Guinea Man. "I already know your story, but why don't you tell the gang?"

Guinea Man nodded and looked around the kitchen at each team member as he spoke. "The Agency burned me. I didn't have a backup, so I staged my death and Vince had some friends willing to move human cargo. I've been hanging out here for the past six months while I work out a new identity and figure out a strategy."

Will cocked his head at Guinea. "What's the holdup? You like playing old man and the sea or what?"

Guinea smiled and looked down at his feet for a moment. "Turns out choosing a name and inventing a back story aren't as easy as I'd thought. I still haven't come up with a name." He looked over at the rest of the team. "You can call me Guinea."

Everyone nodded. It was a reasonable story, and Will could vouch for the guy.

Will took a gulp of his coffee, set the cup on the marble countertop, and then placed both hands firmly on the counter. "Vince has been kidnapped. The Agency gave us bad intel on our last op, and a Russian Mafioso took him somewhere in Saudi Arabia. The Agency buried it and left him twisting in the breeze so we're off the clock and the reservation on this."

Surprise registered on Guinea's face. "Serious?"

Will nodded. "Deadly."

"We've got a contact at the Saudi Embassy who says he can get us some details. This is now our base of operations."

Guinea ran his hand through his black hair. Long locks fell back down into his face. "The Agency is really beginning to piss me off. Its bad enough they burned me but leaving a stand-up guy like Vince hanging out there, well, that's enough to make a man go batshit. Whatever you're doing, count me in. I ain't no stranger to going off the reservation, and I got nothing to lose. I'm a ghost."

Will eyed Guinea. "We aren't negotiating with this guy. We're going in hot and cleaning the scene. You could get worse than burned on this."

Guinea Man smiled and his eyes lit up like two Christmas stars. "Old school style, badass operations. Now *that's* what I'm talking about!"

Will picked up his coffee cup and took a drink. "I think we can use all the operational assistance we can get." He looked around at the team. "Do we want to take some time to talk about this?"

"Nah, I'm cool with bringing him in on it." Jason extended a hand to Guinea who grasped it in a firm handshake. "Any friend of Vince and Will's is good enough for me. I'm Jason. Weapons."

Guinea nodded. "Good to know ya, Jason."

Chris shook Guinea Man's hand and chuckled. "Yeah, it says a lot when a man let's you hang out on his secret island. I'm Chris. Communications and intelligence."

Brian nodded. "Brian. Explosives and anything wet."

Guinea Man smiled with half his mouth. "A tail chasing SEAL, huh? Known a few of your kind. Nice to meet you."

Will pointed to Sarah. "Sarah's been our undercover operative for our last two missions."

Guinea smiled. "And I'll bet you're damned good *under the covers* too."

Sarah shook his hand as she shook her head. The guy was persistent, she had to give him that. "That seems to be the general consensus, but you're just gonna have to take my word for it."

Guinea man shrugged again at the strike out. "You give as good as you get, girlie, and you don't whine about harassment. I like that in a woman."

"All right, people, let's not lose any more time. Guinea, would you show Chris the communications equipment in the office, show Jason to the armory and Brian to the hangar? Sarah and I are going to get ready to meet with Davidson tomorrow."

"Not a problem." Guinea Man refilled his travel mug. "Follow me, guys." He led the way through a door off the living room and Jason, Brian and Chris followed.

Sarah turned and smiled at Will. "You got us a meeting for tomorrow? When did you have time to do that?"

He leaned a hip against the kitchen island and his blue eyes sparkled. "I'm always on the job, pork chop. You got anything formal in that luggage of yours?"

Sarah grinned. "Always. What's the deal?"

Will topped off his coffee cup and looked at the last bit of dark brown liquid in the pot. "I am escorting the Signora Elisabetta Scuro to a party at the American Embassy in Riyadh tomorrow evening."

Sarah handed him her mug. "My alias is having its very own coming out party? Sweet."

He poured the last of the coffee into her cup and placed the empty carafe by the coffee maker. "I had a feeling that alias would come in handy. I'm glad I went with my gut on that one."

Sarah pulled a cigarette from the pack Jason had left on the counter and lit it with the Zippo lying nearby. "So how are we getting to Riyadh—planes, trains, camel caravan?"

"Brian is going to fly us in, and a buddy of mine is hooking us up with a hard car from the airport."

Sarah had never heard that phrase "hard car" before. "Excuse me?"

Will smiled and spoke slowly. "We're going to use Vince's helicopter to fly to Riyadh, and then we'll pick up an armored car at the airport."

"I had no idea Vince even had a helicopter."

"Sweetheart, no self-respecting multi-millionaire with an island in the U.A.E. would be seen without one. Didn't Vince tell you about any of this?"

Millionaire?

Sarah's jaw dropped. "He'd mentioned the island, but I thought he was kidding. The rest of the stuff, well, you know, we really haven't had much time..." Sarah's words trailed off. They'd had enough time for plenty of mind-blowing sex but hadn't talked a whole lot. She began to wonder how much she didn't know about Vince.

"Oh, that reminds me." Will pulled a bank card out of his wallet and handed it to Sarah. "Put this somewhere safe."

She examined the card in her hand. "What is it?"

"The card you'll need to access your money at that bank. Vince and I started the account with the money you gave us from the sale of Hassan's jewels.

Sarah stopped him, confused. "We all worked that mission. It's only right we shared the booty."

Will's blue eyes sparkled. "We're both well fixed, as you can see," he made a sweeping motion with his hand, "so we thought we'd get you started on a fallback plan. It isn't much compared to the estate you just inherited, but it might be good throwing-around money for a shopping trip."

Sarah hugged Will. Tears welled up in her eyes. She didn't try to hold them back. These guys, who had barely known her at the time, cared enough to take the gifts she'd given them and set up an emergency bank account for her. Their thoughtfulness made her heart ache. "Thank you." Tears rolled down her cheeks, but she couldn't stop smiling. "You guys really do take good care of me, and I love you for it."

"That goes both ways, pork chop. You've been doing right by us since day one."

Nine

The two burly men each grabbed one of Vince's elbows and pulled him out of the dark cell. He went along agreeably and eyed his escorts. The fresh air hit him like a slap in the face.

He figured the Australian had about three inches and fifty steroid-infused pounds on him. On a good day, he could take him but he hadn't eaten since Italy, which he figured by his recent loss of appetite was at least three days ago. It wouldn't even be a fight in Vince's weakened condition.

The two men escorted Vince back to the parlor where Nikolai had questioned him the day prior.

At least he thought it had been the previous day. He had no way of knowing for certain what time or even what day it was. They'd taken his watch and his phone when they kidnapped him, and he was still groggy from whatever drug they were using to knock him out.

Good thing we all use code-names for our cell phone directories.

Vince gave a little internal chuckle. It would take a lot more work than anyone was willing to do before they discovered that *Betty,* listed in his cell phone as the waitress from Dave and Buster's, was Sarah. He wondered how she was holding up.

Sunlight streamed through the windows now. Nikolai smiled behind an ornate desk in a large, tan leather chair, twiddling his thumbs and appearing rather pleased with himself.

Vince flopped as his escorts pushed him onto one of the plain wooden chairs in front of the desk.

Ten

Sarah zipped the slit closed on the Ralph Lauren shirtdress. "No sense unsettling the natives with too much thigh showing."

Will called upstairs. "Sarah? Are you ready yet?"

"I'm coming!" She took one last look at herself in the mirror, liked what she saw, and turned to go. She walked out of the closet, which was more of a dressing room given its dimensions. Vince's bedroom suite was total comfort. Oversized glass doors opened to a veranda overlooking the sparkling pool below and the sea beyond. The king sized bed was perfectly outfitted with a down duvet and pillows as soft as sleep itself. The cozy sitting area near the fireplace would be the perfect place to share a nightcap at the end of the day. She smiled and thought this island would be the perfect place for them to get away from everything when this was all done.

I'm bringing Vince back here and we are going to spend a week in this room.

"Hey, darlin', we're headed out to the hangar for preflight. Come on down when you're ready."

"I'm right behind you, Brian." She picked up her garment bag and makeup case and walked downstairs to find Guinea and Chris playing video games on the huge plasma television in the living room. "I should have known Vince would have the largest television known to man along with every game system ever made."

Chris glanced over his shoulder and did a double take with hungry eyes. "It's about time we see you looking your glamorous self again, Sarah. I was beginning to have my doubts. We had a pool going on the sweatpants and ice cream."

Sarah shook her head. "I've got a special bullet set aside for myself in case that day ever comes. You guys and Vince need me to be on the ball. I'm bringing no less than my A-game."

Guinea turned to look at Sarah. "Shit. I ain't never seen an A-game like that. I've been playing in the wrong league."

"Thanks, Guinea." She looked at the big screen and the game Chris had gone back to playing. "Don't you guys have some work to do?"

Chris made a whip snapping sound. "Just taking a short break Mistress Sarah."

She smiled briefly but it faded fast when she considered what she and Will were about to do. "Hopefully, we'll get some good intel from Davidson tonight."

"If anyone can do it, it'll be you and Will."

Sarah turned toward the door. "Thanks. Let's hope so." She walked outside and had her first good look at the grounds of Vince's island. Palm trees were scattered about but there wasn't much to the landscaping from what she could see. The path from the front door led directly to the helipad they'd landed on the night before. Beyond that was a large hangar. Will was sliding the left door open and she could see Brian and Jason rolling a helicopter out.

Damn. Vince really does have a helicopter? What else has he got that I didn't know about?

Of all Sarah's questions, the biggest one at the moment was *what was on the other side of that closed hangar door?* She walked over and peeked around the closed door. A second helicopter, a very big one, waited silently with all but the props hidden under a large tarp. She gasped.

Brian spoke as he rolled the first helicopter out. "Hey! We don't open that door or take that tarp off unless we get confirmation from Chris that there aren't any satellites overhead."

Sarah quickly realized what kind of chopper was under the tarp. The helicopter they were rolling out was a lovely, luxury, civilian helo—the one they'd use to get around. When they went to get Vince, they'd be using the gunship under the tarp.

I just hope he got the ammo to go with it.

Jason appeared out of nowhere and tapped her on her good shoulder as she was about to step into the helicopter. His eyes sparkled as he spoke. "When you get back, I'm going to show you the rumpus room. I think you'll like it."

Eleven

Vince stretched his long legs as he waited in the uncomfortable chair.

Nikolai shuffled through a handful of papers on his desk and then looked up at Vince with a sneer. "I trust your quarters are as comfortable as you expected?"

Vince mustered some sarcasm in spite of his hunger and agitation at being drugged. "Yes, that cot is lovely and the room is very quiet. Very restful. How long should I expect to stay in your Spartan spa?"

Nikolai's sneer melted. "As long as it takes." He picked up a gold pen from his desk and tapped it on his chin. "Now why don't you tell me about Sarah Stevens?"

Vince consciously regulated his breathing. He knew if he appeared anxious, Nikolai would pick up on it, and Sarah would be in even more danger than she already was. "I already told you what I know."

Nikolai remained cool but stopped tapping the pen and pointed it at Vince. "You didn't tell me how you and she met in Italy. Victor told me about his meeting with you and how you had her with you. He said that you met her at a party in Milan. I thought it was an interesting coincidence after our chance meeting in Las Vegas."

"Oh, come on now, Nikolai. You know as well as I do that there is a certain type of woman who appreciates and seeks out the kind of life men like us can provide. We find them in Vegas, Milan, Monaco. They flock to places where power, money, and conspicuous consumption can be found. Don't be naive. Let's stop pussyfooting around, Nikolai. What do you want from me?"

"You're right. I don't need information on Sarah Stevens. She'll be easy enough to pick up and question directly. It seems she was accompanying a gentleman at the Burj al Arab a couple of days ago. She's American and unaccustomed to the culture here in the Middle East."

Vince's heart warmed.

She's here. She's with Will. They know.

"Women go missing here all the time and nobody ever gives them a second thought. It's only a matter of time before my men find her alone and grab her."

Despite Nikolai's certainty that he had the upper hand, Vince's heart grew light with a sudden surge of optimism.

The boys won't let anything happen to her. Leave it to Will to pick up my trail in twenty-four hours or less. That resourceful bastard. I'm going to buy him the biggest, oldest, most expensive bottle of Scotch I can find when this is all over.

Twelve

Sarah watched the activity on the island below as they lifted off.

Within moments, Jason had rolled the little trailer back into the hangar and closed the huge door.

Brian circled the chopper off the island, low and slow.

She noted their flight path against the position of the sun. "Brian, why are we going east when we should be heading west toward Saudi Arabia?"

"I'm flying low and staying off the radar until we get to another island. We'll lift from there so nobody can trace us to Vince's island."

Good plan.

Sarah had been making plenty of mental notes lately about spy craft and covering her tracks. The aliases, the numbered accounts, the dummy corporations for purchasing real estate were all tools they used in their trade that blurred the line between the good guys and bad guys. This was turning out to be her most educational mission yet, but she had a sneaking suspicion she'd only seen the tip of the iceberg.

Will, always with a mind for the mission, turned in his seat to face Sarah. "Okay, so for our purposes, this is just a chopper for hire. Brian has no connection to us and isn't any more than a cab driver."

"Is he taking us all the way in to Riyadh?"

"No, we found some hitches with that plan. He'll take us as far as the airport in Dubai. We'll catch a commuter plane from there into Riyadh and then catch a flight back to Dubai in the morning."

"What time is our plane to Saudi Arabia?"

"Not for a few hours. I noticed you packed lightly so I thought we'd do some shopping in Dubai."

Sarah chuckled. "I'd forgotten how much you like to shop." She nodded. "Sounds good to me."

"Great!" Brian rolled his head for their benefit. "So I get to follow you girls around while you shop and talk about boys?" He clicked his tongue. "Not what I had in mind when I signed on for this gig."

Will rolled his eyes. "We all have our crosses to bear, Brian. You could be stuck escorting La Signora to a stuffy old embassy party."

Brian shook his head. "Jeez. Free booze and hot women in expensive underwear? Throw in a pool and that's my element." He turned to grin at Sarah. "Just another day in the life of Brian, right Sarah?"

Sarah returned his smile and then watched him switch gears from fun loving playboy to super spy as a nearby tower operator called him.

Brian slipped easily into Arabic as he spoke to the tower operator in Dubai. He spoke it so well and with such a perfect accent, that one might believe Arabic was his first language.

That was when it hit her. When he stopped speaking, Sarah had to ask. "Brian? Can I ask you a personal question?"

He seemed to know what she was thinking. "You didn't think I got this great hair from British roots, did you?"

"But your father was a Navy SEAL and your mother is no Arab."

"Dad changed his name from Al Han'ah to Allen when he came to the U.S. The ranch and all that Texas history are on Mom's side of the family."

"But weren't you just a baby when he…"

Brian nodded. "Yeah, but Mom was pretty insistent that I learn the language and culture. I spent a lot of time with his family in Saudi Arabia while I was growing up."

"Good to know." More mental notes ticked away in Sarah's mind.

~~~

The upscale shopping center in Dubai was bustling with people. Every race and color milled about in Arab garb as well as Western style clothing.

Hard to believe we're in the heart of the Arab world.

Sarah made use of her bank card and allowed herself to relax with some power shopping. She took comfort and a sense of security in knowing Will was never far away and clearly on alert. She had just purchased a black silk Ralph Lauren Black Label dress to replace the one she'd ruined on the tarmac as well as some new accessories, fragrances and a few pairs of shoes. Her hands were full of shopping bags as she made her way across the wide, palm-lined hall to the cafe where Will sipped an espresso.

Suddenly a man in traditional white Arab robes appeared from nowhere and stepped in front of her. She tripped, stumbled, and scrambled to catch her bags.

The stranger stopped and looked her in the eye as he handed her a bag that had fallen. "Excuse me, Miss Stevens." He flashed a menacing smile and disappeared into the crowd before Will had time to spring from his table.

Sarah's stomach turned with dread and a chill ripped up her spine.

"Are you all right?" Will grabbed her arm. "My God, what did he say to you? You're white as a sheet."

Sarah barely managed a whisper. "Will, he knew my name!"

Will gripped her tightly with one hand and flipped his phone open with the other. "Okay, let's get out of here." He hit a speed dial on his phone and waited for an answer as they made their way to the exit. "We're coming up to the east entrance. Be there a minute ago."

Brian pulled up to the curb just as Will and Sarah dashed out of the shopping mall.

Sarah opened the door and they both tumbled in without a thought to how they must have looked to other shoppers.

The Mercedes sedan lunged into traffic before Will had even closed his door. Brian checked all the mirrors to see if they were being followed. "What the hell happened in there, Will?"

"Apparently Nikolai was expecting us. Got to hand it to the man, he's got a well-organized operation." Will searched Sarah's shopping bag. "Did he touch you?"

Sarah knew Will was worried about a possible bug. "No. I'm clean."

Satisfied the bag and the goods inside were clear, Will opened his phone and pressed another speed dial number. "Chris, Sarah just got made in the shopping center. You guys make sure you have the security system up twenty-four seven. Keep the place buttoned tight. We're going to travel plan B and Brian is coming to Saudi with us. I'll call you when we get to the embassy."

Thirteen

"Sounds like you have a pretty efficient operation, Nikolai. A small time crew couldn't pull off that sort of legwork. Red Mafia by any chance?"

"We prefer not to use Italian words to describe an establishment so Soviet. It is *bratva*. The brotherhood. Now that you know about my business, perhaps it is time for you to be more forthcoming about yours."

Vince shrugged. "There's nothing to tell really. It is a very small operation. I broker small arms deals and that's about it."

"Oh, please." Nikolai took a long drink of ice water as he eyed Vince. "Don't be so modest. It seems to me that you and Sarah Stevens keep showing up just before my associates start dying. Did you know that Hassan was also an associate of mine? I have it on good authority that he was quite smitten with Miss Stevens, much like Victor was. I find it difficult to believe that is just an unfortunate coincidence. There must be a story to it."

Vince shook his head. "Nope. Just coincidence. It would seem Miss Stevens likes the bad boys."

Nikolai's phone rang. "Excuse me a moment." He pointed to someone standing behind Vince. "Get Vince some cigarettes and something to drink."

A large, beefy hand set a pack of Marlboro Reds, a lighter and a glass of water on the bench next to Vince.

Vince glared at the big Australian. "Thanks, meat."

Nikolai spoke into the phone. "*Da*."

A smile crossed his face. "Shopping? Well done. That should make her nervous enough to bring the others out of the woodwork."

Vince listened intently as he lit his cigarette.

"Are you sure she was with Will Adams?" He smiled at Vince. "Keep me updated." He hung up the phone and chuckled.

Vince remained expressionless as he took a welcome drag off the cigarette and wondered how he could keep the lighter.

Will won't let anything happen to her. She's safe and they're close to finding me.

"Your mother doing some shopping?"

"No, but your girlfriend was. It seems one of my associates *ran* into her. She was with Will. Just another coincidence, I suppose?"

Vince didn't like the way Nikolai emphasized the word "ran." His stomach tied in knots on the inside but he fought to remain calm on the outside. "Really? Well, Will can be bad when he wants to be. After all, a man's got needs, and that woman has a knack for satisfying—if you know what I mean." Vince flashed a wicked grin at Nikolai. "Oh, sorry. You wouldn't know, would you?"

"I wonder how much more you might tell me about your organization if Miss Stevens were here."

A dark cloud rolled through Vince's mind. The thought of Nikolai using her to get information out of him made him sick to his stomach. He knew full well what Nikolai would put Sarah through, and as tough as she was, she'd never be the same afterward. Keeping quiet would kill her but talking would kill them both. Vince hoped he'd never be put in that position.

I can't think like that. Will knows what we're up against. He'll be smart. The boys will take care of Sarah.

Fourteen

"Stop here!" Will grinned as Brian pulled up and parked in front of a small boutique. "Yes." He turned to Sarah before getting out of the car. "Stay here." He turned to Brian. "Keep the doors locked. If they know about Sarah and Vince, they'll know that grabbing Sarah is the key to getting information out of him."

Sarah turned to see if anyone pulled up behind them.

Brian turned in his seat. "Not a problem, Will. I've got some high caliber friends in the front with me."

Sarah had to admit that Brian had style. He always managed to find a way to get a handgun in his hands no matter where he went.

Will stepped out of the sedan, and Sarah heard the doors lock almost instantly.

Like Jason, Brian would make an excellent bodyguard. She wondered why neither of them had gone that career route instead of this one.

Will emerged from the store moments later with two large shopping bags.

The doors unlocked and he slid back into the car just as Brian pulled back out into traffic. It was a well-timed dance, and Sarah marveled at how smoothly they both rolled in this sort of situation.

Will handed one bag to Sarah.

"What's this?"

"Change in plans. We're going native. *When in Rome* and all that shit."

Sarah opened the bag and saw nothing but black. She reached inside. Her shopping skills had refined her sense of touch. Silk, rayon, and a wool blend. She rolled her eyes at Will. "You got me fabric?"

"Abaya and niqab. You can't tell the difference between one woman and another when they're all wearing these."

Sarah shook her head at the convenience and simple genius of it all. Perfect.

Will dropped the other bag into the front seat. "That one is for you. They already saw me with Sarah. If you and she are dressed like the locals, they'll lose her trail and be stuck with me. Better for us to be one target and two defenders than two targets and a bodyguard."

Brian looked into the rear view mirror at Sarah. "Three paces behind me, woman."

"All the better to look at your ass."

Brian grinned. "Oh, baby. You know I love it when you talk naughty."

~~~

After the incident in Dubai, Will called the Burj al Arab and managed to arrange a last minute charter jet to Riyadh, Saudi Arabia. When they landed, Sarah and Will emerged dressed to the nines in formal attire with a natively attired Brian looking the dutiful bodyguard. An armored sedan waited for them at the airport, courtesy of yet another of Will's contacts.

Brian pulled up at the American embassy in Riyadh. "Are you sure you don't want me to go in with you?"

Will plucked a stray hair from his tux. "It's an American embassy, Brian. We'll be checked for weapons when we go in. Better you should stay here and keep those high caliber friends nearby. Just stay alert. Don't pull a Scarface and get distracted by some bimbo in the parking lot."

"Hey now, I only did that once and I was off duty. Nobody got hurt." Brian gazed up at the ceiling of the sedan and rubbed the short beard he'd been growing since he left Las Vegas for the Middle East. "What was her name?" He shook it off. "I got your back." He turned and eyed Sarah from over the front seat. She wore a long, black, low-cut gown that maximized her favorite assets. "You look like a million bucks, Black Betty."

Seeing Brian dressed in traditional robes and headdress and saying something like that just seemed laughable, so Sarah did. "Thanks, Bri. You look like a whole different guy. Whatcha got on under those robes anyway?"

He raised a playful eyebrow. "Wouldn't you like to know?"

"Okay." Will interrupted their flirty banter. "Money time. Let's go find this Davidson guy and get back so we can go get Vince."

Sarah took a deep breath. She'd been trying to keep her mood light, knowing that her stress only stressed the team as well. The knowledge of what Vince might be going through was always there. "Yeah, let's do it."

Sarah and Will made their way through several security stations before strolling into the ballroom. They instinctively paused just inside the door of the sunken room to check the crowd of attendees while they had a height advantage.

Sarah noted the positions of the security cameras covering the ballroom and pointed them out to Will.

"Don't worry, pork chop. So long as there isn't a scene here, nobody is going to review the security camera footage. We'll be long gone before they ever realize we were here."

So much for security.

After a few moments, they walked the three steps down into the ballroom and began looking for Davidson.

Will grabbed two glasses of champagne from a passing waiter's tray and handed one to Sarah.

She sipped the dry, bubbly nectar, anxious to take the edge off. "How are we supposed to find this guy?"

"He said he had our files and would find us if we didn't meet him right away."

Sarah scowled and spoke through her teeth. "Nice. I don't feel so comfortable with that *don't find me, I'll find you* stuff."

Will took a sip from his glass as he scanned the room. "Yeah, I know. Not exactly ideal but it's all we got."

They slowly walked through the ballroom hoping to hear a conversation that identified someone there as Davidson.

Sarah stopped a passing waiter to leave her half-full glass on his tray.

No sense carrying this around. With my luck, somebody will back into me and spill it on my dress. Two ruined designer dresses in two days I don't need.

She looked around and heard a man's voice carrying from a few clusters of people to her left.

"Okay, I've got a great one for you. A horse walks into a bar and the bartender says *'so, what's with the long face?'"* The man grinned and waited for the polite chuckles that finally came.

Luckily for him, a buxom, blond bombshell showed up and took over the crowd. "Speaking of horses, I understand the Prince's stallion has been having a very good season." She looked at the man in robes who was as wide as he was tall. "You must be very pleased."

Sarah tried to ignore the dull conversations and boorish jokes and listened for some reference to Davidson so they could find the guy, get the information they needed and bust Vince out of Nikolai's clutches.

"Are you enjoying the party?" Sarah looked to her left where the voice came from. She smiled a tolerant smile and met the gaze of the horse joke guy. "It's lovely, thank you. And you?"

Will closed the gap and appeared quietly at her side snaking his arm gently around her waist.

His touch and familiar scent reassured her.

The man nodded at Will and then swigged down what was left of his drink in the short, etched crystal glass. "I always enjoy a party."

The buxom blond walked up to the horse joke guy. "Honey, the Ambassador has someone he'd like you to meet. They're over by the East entrance." She straightened his tie and gave him a stern look. "Don't ever tell that joke again."

"What's wrong with the joke?"

The blond just smiled at him like a mother might smile indulgently at a child. "The Ambassador is waiting, darling."

He shook his head and sighed. "Probably some policy wonk." He nodded to Sarah and Will. "If you'll excuse me."

The blond extended a hand to Sarah and grinned as though she were on the pageant circuit. "I'm Buffy."

"Nice to meet you, Buffy. I'm Sarah and this is Will."

"I know. We've been waiting for you." Buffy handed Sarah a calling card. The name on it was 'Buffy Davidson' and there was an address below the name. "Mark and I would love it if you'd join us for a nightcap after the party."

Dread washed over Sarah.

Will took the lead. "Buffy, we were really hoping to get back early tonight. Is there any way we could visit with Mark privately for a few minutes?"

Loud laughter came from the East corner of the ballroom.

Sarah looked over and saw that it was Davidson again, the horse joke guy. She and Will shared a disappointed glance.

"I'm sorry. That just won't be possible here. Meet us at this address after the party. We'll have some drinks and a few laughs."

Sarah's heart sank to the soles of her Manolo Blahniks. She gave Buffy a weak smile and acquiesced with a nod. "We'll see you later then."

Buffy was suddenly distracted like a kitten who'd just spotted a butterfly. "Pamela!"

And she disappeared into the crowd.

Fifteen

Vince was escorted to a large, black marble bathroom where he was allowed to shower at gunpoint. The water washing over him gave his mind pause to escape back to happier times. He remembered the one rainy day he and Sarah spent together in Italy. He'd built a fire in the master suite's fireplace, and they spent the whole day in that room, exploring each other's bodies and making love. It was a very good day.

Vince grabbed the fresh bar of soap. He put it to his nose. It was simple. There was no fragrance, just the smell of clean. A scent he hadn't smelled in several days.

This is just another delay. We'll take care of Nikolai and then Sarah and I can run away and never look back.

After he dried off, Vince wrapped the towel around his waist and ran a hand over his now bearded chin.

How many days has it been?

He looked up at the guard and hoped for the best. "Any chance I could shave too?"

"No blades, mate. We don't invite trouble."

Invite trouble? You stupid son of a bitch, you've already invited more trouble than you can possibly handle. Giving me a blade and letting me walk out the front door is pretty much your only option for survival.

"Looks to me like you've already sent those invitations out, pal."

The Aussie glared at Vince. "You think so?"

A smile curled Vince's lips for the first time in days. "Oh, yeah."

There was a glint of light off metal and pain shot through his head as the Aussie hit him in the face with the butt of his gun and hard steel hit with the force of a baseball bat. He fell to the floor and scrambled to get up, looking around for anything he could use as a weapon. Unless he could pull the toilet from the floor, there was nothing.

The guard tilted his head. "You talk tough for a guy who's about to be in a world of hurt. You want some more?"

"Nah." Vince groaned as he stood and looked in the mirror at his quickly swelling cheek and eye.

No blood, no infection. Could be worse.

"Shaving is overrated." He pulled on his dirty jeans and T-shirt, wishing he could have washed those too, and left the bathroom as instructed by the guard.

The Australian escorted him to a dining room dripping with velvet tapestries where Nikolai waited at a table set for two with gold plates and flatware. Crystal goblets with gold rims sparkled under the crystal chandelier.

Nikolai stared at Vince's face. "Run into some trouble?"

Vince felt the tightness in his swelling cheek as he smiled at Nikolai. "My friend here was just extolling the virtues of growing a beard."

"I'm glad you saw things his way. Any more of that and I couldn't possibly let you dine with me."

"It was hard not to. He had a very convincing argument." Vince moved to the only other place setting at the table, across from Nikolai, and pulled out the chair. "What's for dinner?"

"Why don't we start with a drink?"

Vince tried to stay positive. He knew full well this could be his last supper and there wasn't a damned thing he could do about it. "I'd love one, thanks."

Nikolai motioned to the woman standing in the corner, quiet as a piece of furniture. "Bashira, bring Mr. Hennessee a drink."

Vince had barely noticed the silent woman in the abaya.

She quickly mixed and delivered a vodka martini to Vince. She barely made a sound as she walked across the floor.

Vodka. Should have known.

Vince tried to be kind. Being a servant in this house had to be a miserable existence. "Thank you, Bashira."

She made brief eye contact with Vince and quickly turned away.

That's a fresh bruise on her cheek that'll be a big green lump in a couple days.

"I see we have something in common, Bashira. Is your bruise courtesy of that big Australian brute too?"

Bashira pulled up the face scarf of her plain, black niqab and scurried back to her corner with her head down.

"You really should treat your help better than that, Nikolai. If you aren't careful, they might kill you in your sleep." Vince raised his glass as if to toast the idea and then took a drink of the martini. "Mm, very good. My compliments."

"Thank you. And I'll thank you not to put ridiculous thoughts into the servants' heads. They know what will happen if they step out of line." Nikolai finished his drink in a single gulp. "Vince you've had time to think. I'm sure you've put everything into perspective by now."

"Yeah, I've got perspective."

Bashira replaced Nikolai's empty glass with a fresh martini without even making a footfall on the floor.

Poor thing is probably barefoot.

Nikolai continued as he picked up his drink. "You have an opportunity here. You can be my friend and associate or my enemy. We've done deals in the past, and I've found you to be a very shrewd businessman. As it happens, there has been a recent opening in my organization, as I'm sure you're well aware."

Vince raised his eyebrows. "You want to hire me to replace Victor?" He laughed.

What a mercenary thing to do. Hiring the killer to replace the dead had to be the coldest thing he'd ever been party to. The brotherhood did that though. They respected power, action, and decisiveness.

"Consider it more of a buy-in situation. You can buy into my organization by sharing the information you have such as people, places…well, you know." He smiled.

Vince's stomach turned. Nikolai wanted him to turn traitor.

Of course, he does. If I turn, he gets the credit, and I still get dead. I'm damned if I do and damned if I don't and I know it.

Nikolai spoke as he lit a cigarette. "I would be especially interested in any more information you may have on Sarah Stevens. I thought she and I got along quite well. If everything Victor said is true, she and I could get along even better."

Vince clenched his jaw. The last thing he wanted was this bastard putting his filthy hands on Sarah.

Stay calm. Don't give it away.

"Really? Somehow I don't think she'd be your type. May I?" Vince motioned toward the pack of cigarettes on the table.

Might as well take advantage of every hospitality I can. He's clearly waiting for something.

"Yes, of course." Nikolai pushed the pack toward Vince. "You and Will have established significant contacts in your business dealings. We've seen your operation grow almost exponentially over the past several years. With all of your contacts and the information you could share on Miss Stevens, I'm sure we could come to a profitable, if not amicable agreement."

"You know, Nicolai." Vince paused to light his cigarette. "What I can't figure out is if you connected me with Sarah when Victor told you about her, why didn't you tell him about it?"

Nikolai tilted his head as he looked carefully at Vince. "To be honest, you did me a favor. Victor was becoming a nuisance. He did wonderful business for my organization and even did a considerable business with the United States government, earning us billions over the years. The problem with Victor was that he thought he was bigger than the brotherhood."

Vince leaned back in his chair. "So you were hoping he'd meet an untimely end?"

Nikolai shrugged. "Do you know he had plans to write a book?" He shook his head as though disappointed. "In fact, the manuscript is still out there somewhere. My people are trying to locate it now."

Vince smiled. "What was it about? How to be an arms dealer for dummies?"

Nikolai smiled, he seemed to see the humor in the title Vince offered but the grin disappeared quickly. "He wanted to tell the world about how the brotherhood made its money off the U.S. government. He found irony in the fact that the Soviet Union was ground to dust by the arms race, but the former Soviet republics were being resurrected almost instantly through arms trades and transporting for the U.S. government."

He set his cigarette in the ashtray. "While I'm sure we all see the irony, I don't think I need to explain what such an explosive tell-all would do to one of our most significant income streams." He stubbed out his cigarette in the crystal ashtray and sat back in the large dining chair. "Victor's days were already numbered. When I put you and Sarah together, I decided to wait it out. He didn't know enough to give you anything of value so it was easier and far less expensive to let you take care of him rather than hiring someone myself."

"I see. How did you know we'd take care of him?"

"Please. I'm not a fool. After Hassan, it was too much of a coincidence. Miss Stevens proved herself a Black Widow once again. I have to commend her. Few people would expect so much danger from such a pretty package. She played it very well."

That explains how Nikolai was one step ahead. It's probably a good thing Sarah is retiring. She's already too conspicuous as the glamour girl, although she could be respected in organized crime circles, if she ever wanted to go over to the dark side.

The bruised girl in the abaya entered the room carrying a large tray and began to serve dinner.

Shocked by the sound of his own stomach as it growled, Vince savored the smell of the steak, baked potatoes, and grilled vegetables. He smiled slightly as he wondered what the meal cost Nikolai since none of those items could have possibly been locally grown.

Great. Digesting steak after a couple days of not eating at all is going to be torture. This isn't going to be pretty.

As if reading Vince's mind, Nikolai spoke. "Now we will have a nice dinner and then, you can sleep on your decision in a comfortable bed. What you tell me at breakfast will determine how well you are treated for the duration of your stay, as well as how long your stay may be."

Vince didn't miss his emphasis on the word *stay*. This was a life or death decision.

Sixteen

Sarah ran a brush through her hair as they waited in the sedan outside Davidson's home. "Will, I don't like this. That guy is an ass. And his wife? Please! I'll bet good money she's got more boobs than brains."

Will scowled at Sarah.

She recoiled from his stare. She had never seen him look at anybody that way, and it made every hair on her body stand on end.

"Sarah, you are the last person on this earth who should be judging a woman's brains by her beauty. You're a damned trophy girl if ever I've seen one and trust me, I run in circles that are big on having trophies draped on their arms."

Speechless, Sarah closed her mouth and listened.

Rather than stop, Will barely took a breath as he continued to light into Sarah. "You aren't the only intelligent woman in this world who uses beauty as camouflage. Davidson is our only lead on Vince. If the Agency knew what we were up to, we'd be burned just like Guinea was. We are in no position to be selective here."

Sarah nodded. "Point taken. Hey, why did the Agency burn Guinea anyway?"

"He and his partner were on a mission in South America, and his partner got snatched. The Agency told him to continue with the mission, but he decided to go get his partner first. They still finished the mission, but his handler was a real asshole and burned him anyway."

"What happened to his partner?"

"He retired early and became a contractor."

"Contractor?"

"He runs a major private military company now."

"So does he know Guinea is alive?"

Will grinned. "Oh, yeah. Who do you think helped him fake his death? Brock is the one who sends him his smokes and coffee by the case now."

"That's pretty generous."

"Sarah, when a guy pulls your ass out of a South American prison where you're getting the crap beat out of you every day, you don't think twice about sending him care packages for the rest of his natural life."

"I see your point."

Brian fidgeted in the front seat. "They're ba-ack."

They'd been sitting in the sedan outside the Davidson's house for nearly an hour. After talking to Buffy, both Will and Sarah knew that hanging around the embassy was inviting trouble so they stayed in the car with Brian and drove around the city for a while to be sure they weren't followed.

"Okay, let's go see if they have any information." Will stepped out of the car and held the door for Sarah.

They walked together up the front steps of the grand house and rang the bell.

A maid answered the door.

"Mr. and Mrs. Davidson are expecting us."

"May I tell them who is calling?"

"Mr. Adams."

"And?"

"Just Mr. Adams. This is important so, if you don't mind?"

"Yes, of course, sir." The maid scurried away and left them standing in the front hall of the immense house.

Mark Davidson appeared at the top of the stairs with a smile that seemed to happen mostly on one side of his face. "Hey, there you are! Come on up. We'll have our drinks in the library."

Sarah and Will climbed the stairs quickly and followed Davidson into a large library. Dark wood bookcases lined the walls. Glass doors on all of them protected the aging leather books inside. It appeared to be an impressive collection—likely all at the expense of the State Department. The brown leather furniture set off the dark woodwork and provided a magnificent frame for the most exquisite Persian rug Sarah had ever seen. A small fire burned in the fireplace and rich, sweet cigar smoke scented the air.

"Should I close these doors?" Will was the last one into the room.

Davidson waved a hand nonchalantly. "No, no. Leave it open, please."

"What would you like?" He walked over to the bar at the far end of the room. "We've got everything here, and Buffy makes a mean martini."

Buffy glowed with that pageant smile again.

Sweet Jesus, if I could pull off a smile like that I could rule the world.

"Just Scotch for me. How about you, Sarah?"

"I'll try one of those martinis, thanks."

Will and Sarah sat on the coffee-colored leather sofa and waited for the information they'd come for about Vince's whereabouts.

Buffy brought them their drinks and then said the last thing Sarah expected. "So, are you enjoying your visit to the kingdom?" If the cluelessness was an act, it was a damned good one.

Sarah and Will shared a quizzical glance, and Sarah's mind spun with how ridiculous this couple seemed.

Do these people think we're here on vacation or what? What the hell are we doing here?

Will nodded politely. "Yes, very much. Unfortunately we have pressing business elsewhere and really can't stay."

Davidson stood and walked to the desk. "That's a shame. We're going to the races tomorrow. It's a big social thing here. We'd love to have you join us." He picked up a small box from the desk and turned to face them again. "Will, can I interest you in a cigar? I just received some great Cubans from one of the princes. Too damned many princes in this country, but I really can't complain when they're so generous."

"Don't mind if I do." Will took a cigar from the humidor Davidson offered.

Sarah was becoming unnerved by the small talk and stalling. She crossed her ankles to the left and then to the right.

Will placed a steady hand on her knee. "As much as we'd love to stay for the races, we really do need to hurry back."

"There is some wonderful shopping in Riyadh. Sarah, do you enjoy shopping?"

"Uh, yes."

"You'll have to come back again soon so I can take you to a few of my favorite shops."

What the hell is up with these people?

Will gave Sarah a resigned look and stood.

"Look, I'm sorry. I think there's been a misunderstanding. We meant to meet someone at the party tonight and thought it was you."

Sarah followed his lead. "Thank you very much for the drinks. It was lovely meeting you." She and Will walked toward the door.

Buffy said something in a language that sounded to Sarah as though it could be Greek. In the blink of an eye, two Roman mastiffs appeared in the doorway, complete with bared teeth.

Will put his hand in front of Sarah, gently pushing her behind him, and spoke calmly. "Look, I don't know what you two are up to, but you're making a very big mistake."

Buffy spoke sternly in English this time. "Sit down, Mr. Adams. Sarah, you too." With another foreign command from Buffy, the monsters at the door sat and transformed into adorable but massive puppies. Buffy walked over to them and stepped outside the room.

Sarah sat and fixed Davidson with a glare that promised violence at her first opportunity.

Son of a bitch set us up.

She heard Buffy speaking to someone in the hallway and then soft footsteps walked away. Sarah reached into her purse and held tight to her phone with one finger waiting precariously over number three, her speed dial for Brian.

Buffy reentered the room and nodded at Davidson.

"All clear, sugar lips?"

"She's gone." Buffy nodded and then gave Will and Sarah an apologetic look. "I'm sorry about that. We had to wait until the maid left. We're pretty sure she's a plant." Buffy took a seat on one of the dark leather chairs.

Sarah and Will sighed their relief in unison.

So that's it.

Davidson stood and walked to the desk, unlocked a drawer and pulled a large black and white photo out of it. He handed the photo to Will and sat back in his seat. "That's where he is. It was confirmed this afternoon. As of that time, he was still alive and surprisingly unharmed."

Sarah's breath caught at the thought of Vince being tortured. It was likely to happen. She just hoped they could get to him before it went too far.

Will examined the photo. "Do you know anything about the compound? Any information on security or scheduled comings and goings? Anything else you can give us?"

Davidson shook his head. "That's all I have for now. I've got somebody on the inside working on getting us more information. I'll contact you as soon as I get anything."

Will sat up and examined Davidson. "Why are you doing this? Do you know Vince?"

Davidson shook his head. "I've never met the man in my life. When you get him out, I'll be happy to explain it to him though."

"Good enough." Will stood and shook Davidson's hand. "Thanks for helping us."

Buffy stood and appeared more of a seasoned operative than the ditzy bimbo she'd been earlier. "We'll be in touch. We should have more information for you soon."

Sarah rose and looked at Buffy. She couldn't shake the feeling that she'd seen her before. "Have we met?"

Buffy nodded. "I was a military cop stationed at RAF Lakenheath, too. A dog handler. I left a few months after you arrived. We crossed paths in the armory a few times."

Sarah smiled. "That's it." She shook Buffy's hand and chuckled. "That explains the well-trained dogs, too. Thank you."

"Good luck, Sarah."

Davidson held his handshake with Will. "Let me know if you need anything. I can muster up a few resources if I have to. We need to get him out of there."

"Will do. Thank you, Mark."

Sarah and Will practically ran out the door and down the stairs.

Seventeen

Nikolai walked over to the bar and picked up a crystal decanter. "Would you like a brandy?"

"Sure. Might as well."

Because it may be my last.

Vince sat back in the comfortable dining chair, full from the big meal he'd just eaten. He knew it could be a while before his next meal so he ate as much as he could without hurting himself. He casually took one more of Nikolai's cigarettes.

Stay cool. The more time you can buy, the better the chance of the team getting here before he goes Red Mafia and starts trimming your fingers off.

Vince recalled a young Russian he'd done business with a few years ago. He'd been missing digits above the top knuckle of three consecutive fingers. Vince had assumed it was a grenade throw gone bad, but, after a little too much vodka, the Russian explained how the Red Mafia liked to send messages and persuade people to see things their way.

Vince looked at his hands and then shook off the thought. "So let's talk about this buy-in opportunity you're offering me."

Nikolai returned to the table with two crystal brandy snifters. "Yes, let's talk." His mood seemed more congenial now that Vince was asking questions and showing interest.

The amber liquid sloshed in the wide belly of the glass as Vince accepted it from Nikolai. "Thank you."

Nikolai closed his eyes and inhaled deeply from the fat, round glass. "So what can I tell you?" He settled back into his chair and appeared ready to talk business.

Vince took a sip of brandy and let it warm his mouth before swallowing. "You can start with what you want me to tell you."

"I want the names and cell phone numbers of the other people involved in killing Victor, and I want to know why you targeted him."

"Cell phones? You want to chat with them?"

"You know very well that people can be tracked by their cell phones."

Yes, I do.

"What else do you want?"

Nikolai shook his head and raised his hands slightly. "That's all." He smiled as he sat back in his chair and crossed his legs. "Then you do business as you have been only you're working for my organization. You'll continue to maintain your current clients as well as Victor's. I'll even give you a generous piece of the action. My organization can also offer you protection you don't currently have. After all, if you'd had a competent bodyguard, you wouldn't be here, would you?"

Vince smiled at the irony. "Well, that goes without saying."

Damned if I do and damned if I don't. At least if I don't, the only one who dies is me.

"I think it is time we say good night. Ian, would you please escort our guest to his new room? He has some thinking to do, and I'm sure he'd like his rest."

The big Aussie answered. "Right, Niko. No problem." He nodded his massive head toward the door. "Let's go, mate."

Vince grabbed Nikolai's cigarettes on his way out of the room. "You don't mind, do you, Nikolai?"

"Of course not. Sleep well."

~~~

Vince stumbled into the room with the help of a push from Ian. Golden stucco walls were offset by the red velvet curtains, bedding, and Oriental rug.

Blood red everywhere I look. That doesn't bode well.

The queen-sized brass bed looked inviting and more than comfortable. Any other time he'd be wishing Sarah was here to share it with him. Today he was glad she wasn't. Seeing the bed made Vince suddenly realize how tired he was. After being drugged for several days and sleeping on a small cot, he could almost feel the bed's gravitational pull.

A window.

A flash of hope crossed his mind when he saw the window on the other side of the bed.

Ian didn't move from the doorway. "The bathroom is off to the left there, mate. Don't get any ideas. We stripped it of mirrors so don't go looking for any weapons."

Exposed plumbing could work.

"That window has an alarm and bars so don't even think about opening it. Sweet dreams." The Australian slammed the door as he left and the sound of a deadbolt on the other side ended any thoughts Vince had of busting out.

So much for that. Might as well take advantage of the bathroom and wash these clothes. Nikolai isn't going to like my answer in the morning. I'll probably go back in the cell tomorrow, or worse. At least I can buy a little time for Will to figure this out.

Eighteen

Sarah was the first to walk into the house as Will and Brian were busy tucking the helicopter back into the hangar. She kicked off her Manolo Blahniks and breathed a sigh as her toes dug into the plush living room carpet.

Jason was sitting on the couch, watching Sky News and drinking a cup of coffee.

"Hey, Jase."

He looked up at Sarah while setting the television on mute. "So it went well?"

Guinea called from the kitchen. "Welcome back. You want some coffee, Sarah?"

"Looks like she could use some *tea* and I'm not talking Darjeeling."

Guinea's voice sounded muffled as though he had his head in a cupboard. "I think I have bottle of Cuervo back here somewhere."

Sarah began pacing barefoot in front of the large, marble fireplace, still wearing the long black gown she'd worn to the embassy party. She walked, absent mindedly smoking, and wondering how long it would be before she could pick up a gun and blow Nikolai's head off.

Okay, so it's a little extreme but just when I get the great guy, the house, and the money, some frigging Russian makes off with my man? What the fuck kind of cosmic joke is that?

A voice thundered through the front door. "Chris!"

Jason looked up wide-eyed.

Sarah jumped at the commanding tone of Will's voice. The man never spoke loudly and certainly never yelled. It surprised her that he did now.

Will spoke to nobody in particular. "All right, listen, if Nikolai is as connected as I think he is, we're gonna have a hell of a fight on our hands. We aren't going to be able to do this alone. Guinea, is Brock still running that P.M.C.?"

Sarah mouthed the letters to Jason in the hope he could translate for her. "*P.M.C?*" She'd never heard the acronym before.

Jason flicked an inch-long ash into a nearby ashtray. "Private military company, commonly referred to by the uninitiated as mercenaries."

Sarah opened her eyes wide. She knew they existed but had never met one. She had no idea you could just call them up.

Maybe I went into the wrong business.

Guinea walked out from behind the kitchen island with a bottle of tequila, a shot glass, and a cigarette hanging from his lips. "Old Thunderbunny?" Guinea laughed without dropping the cigarette. "He sure is."

Will tipped his head to one side thoughtfully. "Is he big enough to handle this?"

"Fuck, yeah. He's got a wicked massive operation going. Blackwater has nothing on him."

Will half-smiled. "Good. Where's Chris?"

"He's downstairs running those coordinates you texted." Guinea handed Sarah the bottle of tequila and the glass. "Here's your tea, *Cinderella*."

Sarah frowned at the odd reference, poured some tequila in the glass, and shot it down like a drunk five minutes before last call.

Guinea appeared disappointed. "Gown. No shoes. Missing Prince Charming. Jesus, don't you people read?"

"Guinea, quit screwing around. We need you to put a call in to Brock right away. Use the secure line in the office downstairs. I want a full squad, sixteen guys."

Guinea turned to Will. "Specialties?"

"Marines may be more sympathetic to our cause but mainly we just need sixteen of the meanest motherfuckers in the valley of the shadow of death."

"Hazard pay?"

Will nodded. "Contact is expected. We'll arm, armor and pay top dollar. Have him fax the contract and name his price. I'll transfer the funds immediately. I want his best guys on this."

"When do you want them?"

"See if you can get them here in twenty-four hours. We'll put them up at the Burj Al Arab when they arrive."

"You got it, Billy." Guinea dropped his cigarette in the ashtray and slipped quickly and quietly through the basement door.

"Jason, what's the status of Vince's armory?"

"Weapons all in working order. Plenty for an assault squad. Ammo supplies are all good. Brian's gonna want to check the explosives."

"Has Vince got a Mark-19 in there?"

"Sure does."

"Good. Get one mounted on that chopper and get the minigun set up too. I want a full complement of ammo for both."

"You got it."

Guinea emerged from the basement just as Jason opened the door. "All set. They'll be in Dubai tomorrow night at 2100 hours."

Jason paused to hear Will's plan for the mercenaries.

"Good. I'll call the Burj and get some suites set up on my account. We'll have them standby there until we're ready for them."

Will looked up at Brian who was leaning on the fireplace mantle. "Brian let's get the choppers prepped and ready for action and make sure the explosives are ready."

"You got it, brother."

Jason moved to step downstairs just as Chris returned from the basement with a handful of photos and another handful of notes. He dropped them on the coffee table, plopped onto the couch, and started organizing the photos to create a large satellite picture. He rattled off important tactical information to nobody in particular as he moved the photos around the table.

"I took shots from every angle I could get. The whole place is solid concrete."

The team gathered around the low table to examine the photos.

"The clear area around the compound is two kilometers in every direction. The compound wall is a complete three-sixty with only two gates." He pointed to gates on the East and West sides of the compound. "Here and here. The good news is there are a couple of advisors in the village attached to Jason's old unit." He glanced up at Will. "Maybe we can work that connection?"

Jason seemed thrilled. "Get out!"

"Yeah, any chance you know a Gene Fonseca or Rob Danitz?"

Jason grinned. "Gino and I go way back. He'll help us out."

Will pointed to the basement door. "Make the calls now, Jase. We'll take care of the weapons later."

Jason nodded. "I'll see if I can get the number to Gino's Sat-phone and get in touch."

Brian parked himself on the couch and leaned over the photos Chris had laid out, rubbing his hands in anticipation. "Let's see what we're going to reduce to rubble here."

Will and Chris carefully taped the edges of the photos together to create a large satellite image of the area in and around Nikolai's compound. Satisfied that every edge was in its proper place, Will pulled a cigar from his breast pocket and lit it. He looked around the coffee table at everyone.

"All right, listen. This guy is Red Mafia, and he's bound to have some mean security. We'll need to hit him hard and fast and clean the whole scene. Make no mistake, this won't be pretty."

Brian leaned forward and rested his elbows on his knees. "We're all in, Will. What's the plan?"

"We're going with a time tested technique. Speed, surprise and violence."

~~~

During a break in the tactical planning session, Sarah went upstairs to change into something more comfortable. She returned wearing a pair of jeans and one of Vince's button-down shirts. She walked through the hallway just as Jason came up from the basement. "Have you been on the phone down there this whole time?"

Jason put his arm around Sarah's shoulder as they walked into the living room. "Hey, it ain't easy tracking down a top secret phone number and then hacking into it so your call isn't traced or monitored."

"You did all that?" She stopped and stared with admiration. "Here I thought you were just another pretty face."

Jason smiled and bobbed his eyebrows at Sarah. "That's part of the fun, isn't it? Listen to everything that goes on in planning, kid. Behind the scenes is where the real spy shit happens."

They sat on the floor between the fireplace and the coffee table and examined the notes Brian, Chris, and Will had made on the satellite photo mosaic.

Will looked up from the legal pad he had been furiously scratching notes on. "Jason, what did you get? Tell me something good."

Jason pulled a notepad from his cargo pocket. "Okay, I talked to Gino. They're in. Gino and Rob are up for logistical support but can't get caught doing anything tactical. They have a couple trucks we can use and know a place where we can camp and keep the choppers undetected."

"Excellent." Brian nodded.

Jason handed Will a slip of paper. "These are the coordinates."

Will noted the coordinates on his legal pad and passed the slip of paper to Chris.

Jason continued while Chris took notes. "All we need to do is give Gino a head's up when we're coming in. He'll make sure it's clear. He's got an in with some local Bedouins and will get us a couple tents, about the size of GP Mediums so they'll be big enough for all of us."

"Good work, Jason. Damned lucky you had an in that close. That'll make things much easier. Anything else?"

"Oh, yeah, there's no love or loyalty from the local tribe for Nikolai. They steer clear of his compound for the most part. He pays them off pretty regularly and they take the money, but there won't be any hearts broken if he's blown off the map. Gino is positive Nikolai won't get any backup locally from the Al Han'ah."

Brian sat bolt upright and said the words that were also on the tip of Sarah's tongue. "What did you say?"

Jason gave Brian a blank stare. "What?"

"What's that tribe's name again?"

Jason checked his notes and pointed to the name he'd written. "Al Han'ah."

Little lines creased at the edges of Brian's eyes and he grinned wide as he punched Will in the arm. "Fuckin' ay, Will!"

Will let out a sigh and leaned back against the couch. His crystal blue eyes glowed with the same relief Sarah felt.

Sarah's skin tingled with the possibilities this opened for them. She knew this was exactly what they needed to get the upper hand. She grinned at Brian. *"Me against my brother, me and my brother against our cousin, me, my brother and my cousin against the stranger."*

Brian pointed to Sarah with one hand and to his nose with the other, as if they were playing charades. "That's it!"

Chris laid a curious stare on Brian. "What the hell are you talking about?"

Brian jumped out of his seat and shook his head. "Dude! Have you not read the background information in my dossier?"

Chris stared up at him, confused. "I've read the important stuff." He rattled off bullet points from Brian's resume. "Fifteen years as a SEAL. One of the Navy's best demolition men. Forty some odd successful missions."

"Chris, my father's family name is Al Han'ah. He emigrated from Saudi Arabia."

Guinea snorted. "And this is your intelligence guy?" He chuckled. "Some things never change."

"Hey now." Will sat straight and took a drink from his glass. "Chris doesn't need to know everyone's family history." Will gestured at all the photographic intelligence they had before them. "He does a damned fine job as it is."

Brian smiled an apology and patted Chris on the shoulder. "You're doing fine, man. I don't broadcast my family history for obvious reasons." He checked his watch. "First prayer just finished. I'll make some calls right now. The head of the family is my second cousin, Hamza, so I'll see what information I can get from him." Brian left the room and disappeared down the basement stairway.

Guinea squinted at Will and punctuated his question by pointing with his cigarette between his first two fingers. "Willy, how's a guy with close Arab connections like he seems to have get the kind of clearance needed to do this work?"

Sarah watched Jason's shoulders pull back the way they always did before a fight. She had seen him recoil and spring like a cat when people disrespected his friends. She laid her right hand gently on his knee.

Stay cool, Jase. He doesn't know us.

Will sat back and re-lit his cigar as he eyed Guinea. "Guinea, let me tell you about that man. Brian's father did three tours in Vietnam and even his bones didn't come back from the third one. His mother's family has been ranching in Texas since before it was an independent republic."

"And *commmies* have been living in the U.S. for a century, Billy."

Comparing Brian to a Communist was more than Sarah was willing to stand for. She sprung off the floor. "Now wait a fucking minute!"

Jason grabbed her arm before she could cross the room to Guinea.

"Sarah." Will's brotherly warning and the determined look in his eyes told her he had this under control.

She fumed as Jason pulled her arm, and she lowered herself to the edge of the couch.

Will turned back to Guinea. "Brian passed on a full ride football scholarship at the University of Texas to join the Navy at seventeen. He served fifteen years on the SEAL teams before he was offered this gig." His eyes narrowed. "That man bleeds red, white, and blue."

Guinea held his hands up in surrender. "Okay, then." He turned to Sarah. "My bad. I was out of line."

Will looked around at Chris, Jason and Sarah. "Matter of fact, you could cut any one of my people open and they'd bleed Old Glory for you. You've never seen a greater group of patriots than the folks you're sitting with this morning."

Guinea nodded, quite effectively put in his place by Will's stern words. "That works for me." He stood. "How about some breakfast?"

"Sounds good." Will glanced at his watch and nodded. "We could all use a good meal and some sleep after being up for the last twenty-four hours."

Nineteen

The only sound at the table was the tapping of silverware to plates as everyone dug into the breakfast they'd whipped up together. Scrambled eggs, Canadian bacon, sausage, biscuits, coffee and orange juice were served family style on Vince's large dining room table. In the military tradition, Will laid out a place setting at the head of the table for their missing comrade. It set a somber mood for the team as they prepared to go to war.

Guinea broke the silence. "Hey, I finally thought of a name and a background for the new me."

Brian turned to look at Guinea. "Really? What is it?"

"Anthony Gilbert, former Air Force Security Forces."

Will chuckled. "Okay, man. Tell us what it means."

"My dad was Italian American so I chose Anthony, and my mother's family was Canuk so I chose Gilbert for her. I chose Air Force Security Forces because I now have a new respect for those troops we all used to think were just mindless grunts."

He nodded toward Sarah. "You carry yourself like a professional. It says a lot that you aren't a hysterical mess while we have to wait to get this operation together."

Sarah gave him a half-smile. "Thanks, Guinea."

Brian shot Sarah a wink, and she smiled in thanks for his pep talk at the Burj Al Arab. She wanted to appear the professional Guinea saw, not a sulking mess in sweatpants as Brian had so bluntly put it.

Jason set his fork down and took a drink of his coffee. "So what are your plans for this new identity, Tony? May I call you Tony?"

Guinea tilted his head thoughtfully. "Yeah, Tony is good." He rubbed the stubble on his chin. "I'll probably do some freelancing for Brock for a while just to establish the new identity and get a nest egg saved. Then I'll retire, get myself a little camp up in Maine, and do some fishing."

Jason lit up. "Now that's what I'm talking about." He set his coffee cup down and refilled it. "I don't mind telling you guys, ever since Vince told us he was retiring, I've been thinking about it myself. I've got that log cabin up on Sophie Lake in Montana. Wouldn't be bad to cash in my chips and chill by the lake. There's still plenty of game and big fish up there." He shot a devious look at Sarah. "Maybe I can find myself a good Canadian woman with childbearing hips who can hold her liquor?"

"Yeah the team just wouldn't be the same without the whole gang." Will pushed his empty plate away and leaned back in his chair. "I've been thinking about that too. A man can't keep doing this kind of work forever. I've got that ranch in Venezuela and the only people enjoying it are my wife and the gauchos. The little woman has been quite successful breeding those Polo ponies. Ranch living in South America has its perks." A serene smile overcame his face. He took a deep breath and smiled. "Yeah. What about you, Brian?"

Brian's chest rose and fell with a deep breath. "I could probably put in a few more years just for kicks." He set his fork and knife on his plate and smiled at Sarah. "I think Vince has the right idea. Get a good woman who gives as good as she gets and settle down." His eyes sparkled with mischief. "Maybe I can find myself a scuba diving *mamacita* and kick it in Cabo until my liver gives out."

"I suppose retirement would allow me more time to work on my golf game." Chris ran his fingers through his blond curls. He shrugged. "I do have that friend at Fox News that has been nagging me about taking a consultant position."

Guinea started picking up the dirty dishes. "What about you, Cinderella? Are you and Prince Charming planning on setting up housekeeping here?"

"We really didn't have a chance to talk about where we'd live. Honestly, I really don't care where we go. I just want to find Vince, see for myself that he's all right, and get him back. After that, I can be happy living anywhere and doing anything." Sarah rubbed her face to push back the tears she felt coming. "I'm really tired guys. I think I'll try to get some sleep."

"Yeah, we all need some good downtime. We've got a lot of work to do." Will picked up his legal pad loaded with notes. "I've got a hundred phone calls to make before I sleep." He stood. "Jason, as soon as you wake up, you've got weapons detail. Chris, you'll need to work on that map. Brian, let's get those choppers fueled and mission-ready first thing.

Sarah, we're going to need cots, sleeping bags, and bivouac gear for the desert."

Each of them nodded in receipt of their assignments.

Sarah stood and picked up her dirty dishes. "No problem, Will. Are we going to have enough to feed this army of ours?"

Will's eyebrows rose. "Good question, Sarah."

She shrugged. "Leave it to a former fatty to think about food, huh?"

Brian patted her ass as she walked around the table to the kitchen sink. "*Former* being the operative word."

Will jotted more notes on his pad. "Guinea, when you wake up, check the dry goods stores downstairs and give me a situation report."

"Wilco."

Sarah made for the stairs at a sleepy pace. "Night all."

"Goodnight, Sarah."

"Night."

"G'night."

Twenty

Vince woke to the sound of a key in the door. It was a light touch so he assumed whoever was on the other side was trying to be quiet, but why? He braced himself for the worst.

The door opened and a woman in an abaya and niqab in with a tray of food.

Vince didn't give a second thought to the armed man outside the door when he smelled the fresh eggs and coffee the woman set down on the small bedside table.

She looked up at Vince with the sad eyes of a slave, eyes that showed a spirit battered and just as bruised as her face, most probably all inflicted by ill treatment from her employer.

Vince knew what guys like Nikolai did to people. He also knew they loved hiring sadistic bastards to work for them.

The Australian stepped into the room.

Speak of the devil.

"Nikolai will be out on business for a few hours so you have a little more time to think about his proposal. There's your breakfast. Choke on it." The Australian pushed the woman's shoulder, and she stumbled out of the room.

Bastard.

Vince hopped out of bed as the door closed and pulled on his jeans, which were now both clean and dry. He poured a cup of coffee from the small pot and savored the aroma before drinking the first cup in a single gulp. He picked up the pack of cigarettes and tapped one out, lighting it with the lighter he'd lifted from Nikolai.

How am I going to play this to buy more time? Come on, Will. I won't be able to hold him off long. Should I tell him I'll play ball? If I do, he'll want names and numbers right away. I need to stall.

Twenty-One

Sarah woke with a start to a knock on Vince's bedroom door. Her mind was moving at a breakneck pace immediately. Her voice raspy from too many cigarettes the night before sounded alien to her. "What is it? Is there news?" She jumped out of bed without any thought to what she was wearing and opened the door.

Jason stood there with a serious look on his face. "Okay, sister, you've had eight down. Now it's time to prep for war."

She hugged Jason. "Now you're talkin!" Sarah didn't bother to close the door. These guys had seen her in bikinis and underwear both on the job and off so modesty was a waste of time and energy. She slipped on a pair of jeans and light combat boots and tied the tails of the oxford shirt she'd worn to bed around her waist. She turned to look at Jason as she pulled her hair up into a ponytail. "Let's do it."

Jason led her down to the basement that she hadn't yet had the opportunity to tour. They walked down a narrow staircase and came to an open steel door. Few people understood how Sarah's mind worked. She was thankful that somehow Jason seemed to *get* her, to know that she needed some activity to keep her from focusing on her thoughts—thoughts that would run away with her mind and make her go mad with anxiety over what might be happening to Vince.

Sarah examined the wall as they passed through the door.

One foot of concrete.

"This thing looks like a war pod, built to sustain a serious blast."

"Have you been down here yet?" Jason kept walking. "Welcome to the rumpus room."

Sarah looked around with wonder. She'd seen the guys come down here to use the office but had no idea Vince had the equivalent to a small military base in his basement.

All this is Vince's. I know so little about him.

"No, haven't had a chance. I thought it was just an office."

"Hah! Girl, this is a one-stop war shop!"

Jason pointed to an open door on the left. "That's the armory."

Sarah looked in to see racks of rifles and handguns lining the walls, an arsenal that could easily match any Air Force police armory she'd ever seen. Two large stainless steel islands for gun cleaning and repairs glistened in the center of the room.

Brian was inside packing what looked like bricks of C-4 explosive into a black duffel bag. He looked well rested in jeans and a gray T-shirt that hugged his thickly muscled chest and arms. "Morning, darlin'."

"Hi, Brian. Getting ready for detonation day?"

He grinned and nodded. "Packing party poppers."

She returned his smile. "Nice."

Jason pointed to a door behind Brian. "That door leads to the tunnel that goes up to the hangar. Keeps everything literally on the *down low*." He motioned to a door across the hall from the armory. "That's the office. Secure phone and satellite communications. Chris has been in there taking pictures for hours."

Sarah opened the door and peeked in to see a haggard Chris rubbing his eyes. "Hey, Chris. Have you slept yet?"

Chris rubbed the blond beard growing on his chin. All the guys had gone native and started growing beards when they arrived in Dubai. "Not so much. I'm starting to appreciate the Agency intelligence geeks who usually do our prep work."

Sarah walked into the office, gave him a hug, and playfully ran her fingers through his golden blond curls.

He closed his eyes and seemed to relax for a moment. "Mmm…"

"Hang in there, honey."

He breathed deeply and kept his eyes closed for a moment. "Thanks, doll."

Sarah looked back at Jason. "What else is down here?"

"Storage. Food. Supplies. War gear. Shooting range. Let's go to the armory. I need some help getting the big guns mounted on the choppers. Do you think you can remember your way around a Mark-19?"

Sarah raised an eyebrow and smiled. "Oh, yeah."

Twenty-Two

Vince had been waiting in comfort most of the day until the big Aussie summoned him for another audience with Nikolai. He sat in the chair he'd been shoved into by the Australian.

Nikolai seemed hard at work at his desk, no doubt still tracing the paper trail Victor left the Italian authorities upon his untimely death—when Vince had put a bullet right between his eyes.

When Vince's team had taken Victor out in Italy, the Italian authorities grounded and impounded all of his aircraft that were between flights in Italy. The entire fleet had been down for maintenance so arms dealers and drug dealers around the world were scrambling to find a secondary means of transport.

Vince let a satisfied sigh escape through a smile as he thought about how Nikolai must be taking the brunt of the workload on this one.

Nikolai looked up from the papers he'd been reading. "It seems your busy friends have just—pfft!—fallen off the map." He handed an eight by ten photo to Vince. "That's a very flattering dress on Sarah, isn't it? Isn't that Will with her?"

Vince looked at the photo. Sarah and Will were walking up the steps to a large house, maybe even a mansion. The address was in Arabic so it might be in Saudi Arabia.

State Department, maybe? It couldn't be.

The government would disavow any knowledge of, or relationship with Vince. They were certainly dressed for diplomacy.

A back door source, maybe? Their driver wore traditional robes, but I know Brian's profile, even in a dark photo. The photo is dated. Was it yesterday? They must be close.

Vince's heart warmed and his resolve strengthened. He had every faith they'd find him before it was too late. This photo was all he needed to keep him going.

He took one last look at Sarah in the photo.

Soon.

"Yeah, she's a good looking woman, Nikolai. Too bad you let her get away." He tossed the photo on Nikolai's desk.

"Don't pity me, Vince. I have my best men on it. She'll be coming around sooner than you think."

"I'm looking forward to seeing her again." Vince smiled and meant every word.

"Enough chit-chat." Nikolai tossed the photo aside. "Have you considered my proposal?"

Vince took the cigarette Nikola offered. He paused to light it and take a drag. He squinted through the smoke. "I have." He nodded. "I need some more information before I give you my answer."

"Oh, really? I thought the proposal was quite clear."

"It was when it came to what *I* had to give *you*. It wasn't very clear about what *I'd* get out of the deal."

Nikolai leaned back in the big leather desk chair. "Your cut is simple. You get twenty percent of each transaction. It is the most generous deal I've ever offered anyone."

"It is generous. The thing is I can't quite help but wonder why it is so generous. It sounds a little too good to be true and, in my experience, if it seems too good to be true it probably is."

Nikolai sighed and leaned his elbows on the desk in front of him. He leaned forward and his voice dropped slightly.

"It is so generous because you have something of high value to me and because torture is so *Cold War*. I'm progressive. I would rather motivate in a positive manner and give you a reason to come into business willingly rather than grudgingly." He tilted his head slightly. "There is no reason we can't be friends, Vince."

"Well, then you won't mind me taking another night to think about it."

"Of course not. Just realize that if my men find Sarah before you and I set a deal, my offer will be withdrawn. You may want to consider taking me up on it now while you still have something to bring to the table."

Vince stubbed out the stump of a cigarette. "I understand."

Nikolai motioned to the Aussie. "Please take our guest back to his room and see that he has a good dinner." Nikolai nodded to Vince and spoke more of an order than a request. "If you'll excuse me, I have work to do."

Vince grinned wide. "I suppose the Italian authorities' seizure of everything in Victor's office has set your bookkeeping back a bit, huh?"

Nikolai glared at Vince. "Get out."

Vince reveled in the satisfaction of knowing he'd inconvenienced Nikolai if only just a little and stood to leave. "No problem."

Twenty-Three

Sarah slung two spare barrels over her shoulder and hefted two M-60 machine guns through the tunnel following Jason, who carried a Mark-19 automatic grenade launcher and the helicopter mount.

Sarah and Jason had become regular drinking buddies between missions when they were living in Las Vegas. Jason liked to get into the posh clubs and having Sarah on his arm made it possible. Sarah liked to go slumming every once in a while and just hang out at a dive bar shooting pool. Having Jason with her always put her on the winning side in any brawls that broke out.

Jason was also her sparring partner and *sensei* of sorts in her fighting training. She was used to Jason being the muscle, especially when they got into bar brawls, but she was still impressed that he could throw a seventy-five pound gun over his shoulder and walk at a steady clip without leaning. She was suddenly aware of how very physically, financially and intellectually powerful her friends were and considered herself lucky to be a part of their little family.

At the end of the tunnel, they came to an elevator.

"This stuff isn't cheap, Jase. Where did Vince get the money for all this?"

Jason pushed the button for the elevator. "Sarah, no self respecting arms dealer could hold his head up in the international underworld without a setup like this. It's all trappings of the trade."

"So the Agency paid for all this?"

"In a manner of speaking. The Agency doesn't like to sign off on stuff like this. Generally, you need to set up your sales to go to two different accounts. One account belongs to the Agency and the other to you."

They stepped on to the elevator. "So it is standard operating procedure to skim?"

Jason pressed the elevator button. "In a word? Hell, yeah."

The floor of the hangar above them opened up and they found themselves at the far back of the hangar. Jason set the Mark-19 on the clean, polished floor near several, neatly stacked, black canvas bags. "Just leave those here for now."

Sarah stared at the guns and the bags of explosives and ammo. Something clicked in her head and she stopped. Dread swept over her like a cold breeze and she shivered.

Even these aren't guarantees of Vince's safety.

She croaked through the frog in her throat. "Jason?"

Jason turned to face her. "Yeah?"

"Are we going to be able to do this?"

He grinned and his eyes wrinkled with laughter. "Any monkey, even an Air Force cop like you, can mount an M-60 to a chopper, Sarah."

Sarah found no humor in the joke today. Her shoulders sank, and she shook her head. "That's not what I'm talking about."

The laughter left his hazel eyes. His voice dropped a little deeper like it always did when he was serious, which wasn't very often. "I know, Sarah." He grabbed her shoulders and looked her in the eyes. "Never, ever allow room for doubt in your head, your heart, or your gut. We've got the best equipment and people in the business right here on this little sandbar. Always remember, *who dares, wins.*"

"Where have I heard that before?"

"Okay, so it wasn't original but it is appropriate. It's the British SAS motto and it's every bit the truth. Have you ever heard of the SAS failing, at *anything*?"

Sarah gulped back the frog in her throat. "No."

"Exactly." Jason shook her shoulders just enough to make his point but not enough to agitate her nearly healed gunshot wound. "We're the heroes, Sarah. Don't forget it. We're going to save Vince, kill the bad guys and then we'll all live happily ever after."

Sarah wanted to cry and hated herself for it. She trusted Jason and needed his reassurance now as much as she needed to breathe. "How can you be so sure?"

Jason placed his hands on either side of Sarah's head and pulled her close until their foreheads touched and their eyes were just inches apart. "Because the alternative is unacceptable and because we have this…" He wrapped an arm around Sarah's waist and led her over to the covered helicopter and pulled the tarp away from the nose with a flourish. "Ta-da!"

"Jesus, Jason!" Sarah nearly squealed with excitement as she moved forward for a closer look. "Is that...?"

Jason walked around the helicopter, carefully removing the rest of the huge tarp. His muscled chest puffed up with pride, and his voice was clear and confident as he described what Sarah was looking at. "That's right. Sikorsky's finest. The MH-60L Direct Action Penetrator. Civilians just call it a Blackhawk helicopter but this bad boy has some special operations modifications." He walked around the helicopter and pointed them out. "We've got Hellfire missiles with a maximum range of five miles." He patted the barrel of a Gatling gun. "We've also got two M134D Gatling guns mounted as door guns."

Sarah marveled at the fact that a civilian could acquire such a devastating piece of war machinery. "This is amazing!" She bounced up and down on her toes as a new optimism cleared the doubts from her mind for good.

Jason began spreading the huge tarp out on the floor of the hangar. "I'm glad you're impressed. You helped us get a discount on this one. The day Vince dropped you off at Victor's place he got a hundred thousand off the selling price."

Sarah's eyes opened wide. "I was worth a hundred thousand?"

Jason eyed her with disbelief. "You aren't the fat girl any more, Sarah. Women like you go for way more than that on the black market. If you were mine, I wouldn't part with you for any less than a cool million and a hard fight."

Her heart warmed. Jason wasn't normally a demonstrative guy, but the look in his eyes as he watched her told her he really meant that. Other women would be offended, but when your job is sleeping with bad guys for secrets, you like knowing your rate is a good one.

Not one to be serious for long, Jason rolled his eyes. "Now put your inflated ego away and help me fold this mother."

Sarah took a deep breath and set to work. Time flew as they loaded ammunition and gear into the Blackhawk. The physical work helped Sarah to feel productive, like they were getting closer to finding Vince.

Jason stretched. "How about some chow?"

Sarah looked up from the ammunition she was loading into the chopper. "Who, me? Always."

He smirked in his Cheshire cat way. "We can't go into an operation with low blood sugar now, can we?"

They walked through the tunnel and back into the basement where Brian and Guinea were packing bags of war gear. Tactical vests, bulletproof vests, belts, and holsters were counted and packed into big black canvas bags.

Will and Chris were in the office checking maps, coordinates, and schedules.

Jason poked his head into the armory. "Who's cooking tonight?"

Sarah knew full well he who asks gets the task and suspected it was a rhetorical question on his part.

Guinea looked up. "I put some cold cuts in the fridge this morning. There are some sandwich buns on the kitchen counter."

"Cool, come on, Sarah. Let's go make some sandwiches."

Sarah followed Jason up the stairs.

"Stevens!"

Sarah stopped at the sound of Will's voice but didn't turn around on the stairs. "Yeah?"

"Telephone."

Sarah hot footed down the stairs. Will handed Sarah the handset attached to the secure line in the office. "It's Buffy Davidson. They want a face-to-face."

Sarah realized Mark Davidson would be under constant surveillance due to his position as a political attaché. The only way they could do a face-to-face meeting was with Buffy. It made sense for her to meet with a woman rather than raise suspicions by meeting with a man. Sarah wondered why they had to do a face-to-face at all when they had a secure telephone line and Nikolai's people were already on the lookout for Sarah. "Hello?"

"Sarah, it's Buffy. We gave all the details to Will. You and I are going to meet for a shopping trip."

"Thanks, Buffy, but the last thing I want to do is shop. Can't you just give us the intel we need right now? We aren't here on vacation."

Buffy's voice was terse. "I realize that, Sarah."

Sarah's patience slipped away like sand through an hourglass. "We can't expect Nikolai to just keep Vince as a houseguest. Do you understand that lives are in the balance here? What if it were Mark? Wouldn't you want to handle it quickly?"

"Sarah, you misunderstand. Of course, I would want to handle it quickly, but more importantly, I'd want to do it right. Just meet me in Dubai."

Twenty-Four

Sarah observed Buffy from across the table. She appeared so plain in the abaya without makeup or her lovely, long blond hair showing. Sarah realized that was the point. They were both in abayas and with all the glamorously clad women milling about, two women in traditional garb blended into the background just as well as two palm trees might.

Buffy's eyes were intent as she spoke in hushed tones. "Two women go in and out of Nikolai's compound daily. One is the cook and the other is the maid. They always travel together. They live in the nearby village. Their family name is Al Han'ah."

Sarah didn't waste time asking where the information came from. Buffy wouldn't risk the meeting if the Davidsons didn't believe their source was good.

Brian walked up wearing the white robes Will had bought and sat to read a newspaper at the table next to them. He nodded at Sarah before opening his paper.

His meeting with the newly arrived mercenaries called in to assist in their rescue of Vince must have gone well. He smiled as he read an Arabic newspaper and watched Sarah from the corner of his eye.

Buffy slid an eight by ten photo across the table to Sarah. "As you can see from the satellite image, Nikolai's compound is surrounded by wide open desert. There is a small village to the northeast, about two clicks away."

Buffy may have traded in her battle dress uniform for designer labels, but she still talked like a military cop.

"Every morning, mother and daughter Al Han'ah," she pointed to the back gate, "enter through this gate and go inside to do the cooking and cleaning for the day. They leave every evening just after sundown." She leaned forward and lowered her voice even more. "Now this is your operation and I haven't been tactical since my military police days, but I see some definite possibilities here."

Sarah knew exactly what she meant and nodded. If they could get the women to cooperate, Sarah could go in as one of them to recon the compound and make sure Vince was still there.

Buffy passed Sarah a manila envelope. "Here is the dossier we have on the Al Han'ahs."

Twenty-Five

Sarah lounged on the long semicircular couch facing the fireplace and watched Chris as he worked. Vince had been missing five days now. They'd come a long way toward getting him back, but they still had much more to do.

Chris sat cross-legged on the floor and made more notes on the satellite photo mosaic of Nikolai's compound, the surrounding area, and the nearby village. He'd made notes of all the GPS coordinates of every structure, door, and well. He'd even noted the current moon phase, which was due to be new in two days. A dark moon would be the perfect opportunity for a night attack.

Sarah and Jason waited quietly as Will wrote on his notepad, Chris made notes on the makeshift map, and Brian made phone calls downstairs.

Guinea walked in with a fresh carafe of coffee and set it down on the only uncluttered spot on the coffee table. "Damn, Chris, you may suck at history but you are totally obsessive when it comes to all that science and math stuff. I'm impressed."

"Thanks, Guinea. Good to know I have one or two redeeming qualities."

Will copied the coordinates onto his notepad from the photo Buffy had given Sarah and then passed them to Chris so he could compare them to the ones they'd taken.

Sarah wasn't used to sitting still, and she hadn't caught up on all her lost sleep. She nodded off but jolted from her doze when she heard Brian bounding up the stairs in what must have been three at a time. He appeared at the basement door after only three stomps.

He was smiling wide. "We're all set!"

"Send it, brother!" Will had a hopeful look on his face. "Whatcha got?"

Brian sat on the couch and grinned. "Jason's source was right on. Nikolai hasn't made any friends out there. The ladies are distant cousins, *very distant*, but I used to play soccer with the old lady's son. It seems Nikolai's man hasn't been treating the ladies so well, and Hamza would be happy to find any excuse to have Nikolai either run through or run out of town." Brian looked at Sarah. "I'm not suggesting this as a plan of action, but if we wanted to have one of the women take a day or two off, they wouldn't be averse to it. Just sayin'."

Sarah nodded and sat up straight on the couch. "I was thinking the same thing. Will, you know we need interior reconnaissance. We shouldn't go in blind. Nobody will be the wiser when I'm wearing an abaya and a niqab to cover my hair and face. Let's do it!"

Will gave Sarah a questioning look. "Are you sure?"

"Do you even have to ask?"

Will shook his head. "All right, here's how we're gonna play it. It's too late to get everyone in place tonight. Brian, you talk to your cousins and set it up so Sarah goes in the day after tomorrow. When you get that done, get with Chris and Jason and start plotting our flight plans. I want the choppers to take separate routes. We'll take off at dusk tomorrow. Jason, are you still good to fly the gunship?"

"You bet your balls I am."

Brian dashed downstairs to make his calls.

"Good. When you get the flight plan settled, make the call to your boy Gino. Tell him we're going to need a good place to camp and those tents he mentioned. And we'll need a truck waiting at the landing zone to get Sarah to the village for work. Once you get all that together, get some sleep."

"You got it. What about personal weapons?"

"Arm up and load the choppers with handguns and rifles for every man before we go. Everything in that armory mission ready?"

"Affirmative." Jason left the room and disappeared downstairs.

"Good. I'll put a call in to Davidson." Will turned to Sarah. "Sarah, have you still got that palette of colored contacts we bought for you back in Vegas?"

"Sure do."

"Great. You'll need brown eyes. Those green ones of yours will draw too much attention. Get some of that self tanner I know you have and get to work on your face. You'll need to be darker around your eyes if you're going to pull this off."

Twenty-Six

The sun was nearly down on Vince's sixth day in captivity when Sarah and the boys checked their personal gear in the hangar before loading the choppers and moving out. They looked like a real force to be reckoned with in black battle fatigues and T-shirts with handguns strapped to their thighs and extra ammo clips on their belts.

Will broke the silence. "All right, troops, this is it. This is the point of no return. We're about to declare war on the Russian Mafia on Saudi soil. If we get caught, there are only two possibilities—either the Russians will kill us or the Saudis will. If you aren't up for it say so now. If you're in, you're *all* in. There can be no turning back from here."

Sarah tucked her Ka-Bar into her right combat boot then checked the ammo in her Sig Sauer SAS forty-fives and holstered them in their thigh holsters. "Will?"

"Yeah, Sarah?"

"Quit flappin' your gums and check your gear. We've got some ass to kick and not time to waste."

Will beamed and shook his head. "Right on, sister." He finished loading his gear into the civilian chopper and walked over to Jason, who was checking the Blackhawk's systems before takeoff. "You all set, Jason?"

Jason looked up at Will. "Right as rain. I've got Chris on navigation and Sarah and Guinea on guns."

Sarah and Guinea, both ready for action, grunted, "Hooah!" in unison.

Will's face blanched. "Jason, you have to get in there with no contact. We can't afford any target shooting. Sarah, Guinea, any contact before we get to the rendezvous point will compromise our mission. Jason, you need to avoid any possible witnesses."

Jason put a calming hand on Will's shoulder. "We're good, Will. I was kidding. This isn't my first rodeo, you know."

Will looked down at his legal pad and rubbed his forehead. "Yeah, you're right. I'm sorry, man."

"It's okay. You're a great leader. You've covered all the bases. It's a good plan, and we're going to nail it just like we did on the tabletop run-through."

Brian swaggered over to Jason with a shit-eating grin. "Feels good to be back in the cockpit, doesn't it?"

Jason beamed. "You know it."

Will patted the doorframe. "You sure she isn't too much for you to handle?"

"Are you kidding me? I've been making love to this old girl for years. She's the same model we used in the Army. It's the real women I can't handle. They got no instrument panel."

Brian gave Jason a fist bump.

"You're true blue, Jase."

"Nah, I'm O.D. green. Blue is for pussies like you." He turned to get into the cockpit. "See you at the party."

Sarah and Guinea climbed into the gunners' seats of the Blackhawk and buckled in.

"You got it." Brian walked over to the closed hangar doors and prepared to slide them open. His voice carried clearly through the hangar. "Ready, Chris?"

Chris sat in the copilot's seat of the Blackhawk. "Not yet." He gave Brian the hand signal to stop and watched his laptop screen for a window when satellites wouldn't be passing overhead while Jason fired up the war machine for a speedy egress. Within just a few seconds, Chris flashed Brian the all clear with a thumbs up, and Brian and Will threw the massive doors open swiftly.

Sarah felt the Blackhawk lift just slightly and then they flew out of the hangar as though Jason did this sort of thing every day. She smiled with pride.

Sometimes I forget just how amazing my friends really are.

Sarah took a deep breath, relieved they were finally underway.

We can do this. We can do anything.

She went over the plan in her head. Brian and Will would stop at the Burj Al Arab to pick up eight of Brock's guys and Will's pilot friend, Leo, would pick up the other eight. The two helicopters would take different routes to the rendezvous point and arrive approximately ten minutes apart. The team in the Blackhawk, consisting of Jason, Chris, Guinea, and Sarah, would take a third route, specifically designed to bypass any even remotely populated areas. They would arrive shortly after the other two choppers.

The setting sun cast a red glow over the desert beneath them. *So clean, so smooth, so fluid in the wind.* Dunes passed like waves in an ocean of sand. They flew at 175 miles per hour over a crystal ocean of red sand tinted by the last rays of the sun. Peace settled over her. In that moment she understood how the Bedouins could live the nomadic lives they did.

The desert is so pristine, so pure.

The dark waves of sand lulled her into a meditative state. She saw Vince. She saw every step of the operation, and she saw them all leaving safely and going back to their lives as planned. It would happen. She knew it would. Secure in her own training and the combat experience of her team, Sarah closed her eyes and let sleep take her.

~~~

Jason set the Blackhawk down in a small, deep valley just big enough for three choppers, two big, black Bedouin tents, and two small pickup trucks. Jason's buddy, Gino, had come through with the gear.

Sarah scanned the area. The small valley was surrounded by high dunes. If they were seen by satellites, nobody would think they were anything more than another Bedouin family making camp.

The civilian chopper flown earlier by Brian and Will was covered with desert camouflage so as not to arouse suspicion from anyone flying overhead.

Jason landed the Blackhawk and shut down the rotors. Will and two big guys wearing desert camouflage ran out of a tent with a huge roll of camouflage netting. They used a couple of long poles to stretch it over the Blackhawk. A couple big guys wearing dress slacks and oxford shirts stepped outside the tent and lit cigarettes. Sarah was happy to see the mercenaries dressed appropriately for the Burj al Arab. No doubt, they'd all be changing into their preferred combat garb soon.

Sarah stretched from her catnap.

Jason removed his helmet and looked back toward Sarah and Guinea in the gunner seats. "We'll need to stay under cover in the tents as much as possible and stay inside when satellites are passing. Chris will be tracking them in real time."

Chris nodded and closed his laptop. "Looks like we're clear for another twenty minutes."

"Perfect." Jason opened his door and stepped out.

Chris, Sarah, and Guinea followed.

Jason's face lit up as he walked toward one of the big guys busy draping the camouflage netting over the chopper.

Guinea grabbed the camo netting and continued the task as the big guy greeted Jason with a smile and a man-hug.

Jason grinned from ear to ear. "I never thought I'd see your ugly spaghetti-eatin' face again but I'm glad I did."

"Well, hell, man. I've been playing in the sandbox all this time. Heard you got picked up by the Agency. I see it hasn't improved your standard of living."

"You'd be surprised!" Jason laughed and patted him on the back. "Did you meet the crew yet?"

The man motioned toward the tent. "Yeah, the squad of mercs in there and the two Navy guys." He saw Sarah and stared. "Who have you got with you here?"

Jason made his introductions. "This is Chris, Guinea and Sarah. Guys, meet Gino."

Gino shook Chris and Guinea's hands and then fixed Sarah with a questioning look. "What's with the broad?"

Jason gave Sarah a wink and then turned back to Gino. "The *broad* is cool, just don't piss her off. And stay out of arm's reach plus about six inches. She's got a body count."

"Always with the jokes! Come on, you are pulling my leg?"

Sarah took a deep breath and sighed. She glanced at her watch. "As much fun as it might be to stand around and bullshit, we've got a satellite coming." She shot Gino a perfunctory smile. "Nice to meet you, Gino. Thanks for helping us out." She started walking toward the big, black tent and overheard Gino's words.

"She'd be hot if she didn't talk."

Jason chuckled. "Same old Gino. Trust me. She's hot no matter what she does."

Sarah stopped as she stepped inside the tent. She was struck by the sweet scent of Frankincense. She couldn't resist sniffing the woolen curtain serving as a door. The scent was in the fabric from years of absorbing the smoke from the Bedouins. The next scent to draw her attention was the mix of coffee and chai. Fluorescent, battery-operated lanterns lit every corner of the room. Two dellas, large brass coffee pots, sat in glowing coals in a large, shallow metal box in the center of the tent. Persian rugs covered the sand floor and made for a comfortable camp. Impressed with the service, Sarah grinned. Any other time, this might be a fun getaway with friends.

She glanced around the room at the men sitting on or reclining on bags of gear, drinking coffee and chai from glasses in silver holders. These were the mercenaries, or rather contractors, Guinea's friend Brock sent them. All muscular and fit, they sported short haircuts and those with facial hair kept it well trimmed. She had to hand it to Brock, he didn't send any slobs.

The room went silent when the mercs noticed her. She took a deep breath and smiled. "Thanks for coming, boys."

Three men in traditional white robes standing just inside the tent to Sarah's left, spoke animatedly in Arabic and gestured to Brian who was smiling like a Cheshire cat.

He waved Sarah over.

Sarah strolled over to Brian. He introduced her to his kinsmen in Arabic. "Hamza, Abdullah and Muhammad, I want you to meet a very special woman. This is my friend Sarah. Don't let her beauty fool you. She fights as well as any man I know."

The men appeared skeptical and seemed to size her up.

Sarah spoke in Arabic for their convenience. "Thank you, Brian." She smiled and nodded politely to the men. "It is my pleasure to meet Brian's family."

When they looked to Brian again, he nodded to reassure them this wasn't a joke.

Sarah had expected this sort of response and watched their faces as they tried to wrap their brains around such a compliment to a woman.

Brian continued to speak Arabic like a native. "My kinsmen collected rugs, coffee and chai supplies to welcome us in style."

Sarah smiled and bowed her head slightly to the men, genuinely grateful. "Thank you very much for such a gracious welcome. We are indebted to you for your generous assistance to help our friend."

The one Brian introduced as Hamza smiled politely. "The welcome was the least we could do for our cousin. It has been too long since we have seen him. For your friend, may Allah will watch over Vince until we can make the Russian answer for what he has done."

Sarah touched her right hand to her heart and replied with a heartfelt. *"Inshallah."*

From your lips to Allah's ears.

She looked for a reason to excuse herself because her sex and knowledge of Arabic really seemed to boggle these guys. She couldn't blame them.

How many Arabs have seen a woman in battle dress with forty-fives strapped to her thighs who can speak Arabic? Probably only three.

She noticed Chris in a corner setting up his small satellite and laptop rig.

"Chris looks like he could use some help. Would you excuse me, please?"

The men nodded and then whispered to Brian.

She shook her head as she heard him answering in the affirmative.

"Let's have some chai, and I'll tell you some stories."

I really hope he doesn't tell them the embarrassing ones. God knows he's got a few.

Sarah was helping Chris set up and check his communications equipment when Will stepped inside the tent and whistled for everyone's attention.

The room went silent.

"Okay, gentlemen, I want to thank you for your patience in waiting for a mission brief. I'm going to give you a preliminary, informative briefing tonight and then we should have enough details for a mission briefing tomorrow night."

Everyone focused intently on Will.

"First, I want to reiterate that this is *not* a sanctioned operation in any way, shape or form. We have a friend, a former Force Recon Marine…" The sound of half the room saying, "*Hooah!*" interrupted Will. He looked up at the men and smiled. "Excellent. As I was saying, our friend has been kidnapped by a fellow who lives, but isn't entirely welcome, in these parts. While this mission isn't sanctioned by any government, we have the full support of the local population and our Bedouin hosts who are, by the way, the folks we owe our thanks for the tents, coffee and chai."

The men raised their glasses and mumbled their thanks before turning back to focus on Will.

"This tent will be our day-room for chow and, sorry to say, standing by."

Sarah had to hand it to the mercs. They were real pros because not one let out a peep about having to wait around in a tent in the middle of nowhere.

"The other tent will be used for sleeping. There is a field latrine on the West wall."

A lanky blond with a high and tight haircut spoke up. "Any idea when we'll engage? I'd hate to waste y'all's money just sittin' around."

Will pointed to Sarah sitting near Chris. "If Sarah can get us the intel we need tomorrow, we'll have an attack plan to raze the Russian's compound the next night, and have you all out of here on first class tickets on day three."

Gino leaned in and whispered something to Will.

Will nodded. "Sarah is going in tomorrow morning to locate Vince and do a recon of the compound. With any luck, she'll be back tomorrow night with the intel to plan the attack. Until then, get plenty of rest and stay under cover. If you have any questions, find me, or Brian, the tall guy with the tan."

Brian gave a brief wave to identify himself.

"You can also find Chris, the guy with the computer, or Jason, the guy over there with the weapons and the crazy look in his eyes."

Jason looked up from an M16 rifle he was function checking. His cigarette hung from his lip and he smiled a half smile.

"We've got MREs and water for everyone over there." Will pointed to the far corner of the tent stacked with cases of water and military-style meals ready to eat. "Carry on."

Twenty-Seven

Just a sliver of a moon made eerie shadows in the camp as Sarah walked to the Blackhawk and grabbed her small duffel bag packed with abayas and a set of Kunai throwing knives. She slipped one of the abayas over her T-shirt and black battle dress pants and left the SIG 45s on her thighs. Brian and Gino pulled the camouflage netting off one of the trucks. Hamza and Brian's other two cousins hopped in the back while Sarah sat in the front between Brian and Gino.

After driving about a mile and a half on what could barely pass as a path, Gino broke the silence. "Are you sure you know what you're getting yourself into, girl? Those Russians play for keeps."

Great. Yet another chauvinist pig. I'm so tired of dealing with these macho fuckers.

Sarah would never get used to being underestimated by everyone she met. She knew Gino had helped them out, but his tone was like fingernails on a chalkboard. "I appreciate what you've done for us, but this isn't a game and I'm not playing."

Brian interrupted before the conversation degraded any further. "Gino, I was on the SEAL teams for fifteen years so I get where you're coming from, but Sarah's been trained by some of the best, including Jason, and has some pretty impressive operational experience. I'd trust her to have my back no matter what goes down."

"That's cool but can she handle going in undercover like this? From what I hear, this guy isn't very good to the help."

Sarah stopped Brian before he continued. "Thanks, Brian, but I don't need you to defend me to this guy." Sarah turned to Gino. She was ready to pop and this guy looked like he could take it.

"I am not *playing* spy here, I *am* one. I'm not some JEEP just out of training hot-dogging it. This is what I do, and I seem to have done it pretty well up to now because I'm sitting here in this truck with you and not six feet under."

Gino seemed to inch away from Sarah and closer to the driver's side door.

She lifted the skirt of her abaya. "In case you're wondering, these are 45s strapped to my thighs, they're loaded, and I know full well how to use them."

Gino shot a confused look at Brian.

Sarah never took her eyes off Gino's face. "I'll also carry three kunai knives strapped to each calf when I go in. Nine times out of ten, I hit my mark even with distractions. So, yeah, I know what I'm getting into. Thanks."

Gino appeared confused and looked across Sarah to Brian as though he couldn't believe it unless a man said it.

Brian nodded. "I tried to tell you. She's the real deal, man. Do us both a favor and don't piss her off again."

"Good enough." Gino drove the rest of the way in silence.

They traveled into a small town that was more a collection of small, walled compounds. Dogs barked in the dark and a dust devil would spin up in the headlights every few minutes but there were no people to be seen.

Gino pulled up to one of the concrete walls and everyone exited the truck.

Sarah sighed with relief to be out of the cramped cab, so close to someone she could easily take her frustrations out on.

Abdullah, one of Brian's cousins who'd ridden in the back of the truck, led them to a door around the side of the small walled compound. He opened the door and bowed slightly to Hamza who walked in first.

Sarah watched as the family politics played out in the small parade. First Hamza, then Brian and Sarah, followed by Gino, Muhammad, and Abdullah.

Sarah took a visual stock of the small dusty yard. Date, olive, and citrus trees, a small henhouse and a large water tank—all things necessary for survival in Saudi Arabia's Empty Quarter—were laid out around a concrete patio. The chickens were quiet but a Saluki dog trotted out of the shadows and nudged Hamza's hand with his nose. Hamza rubbed the dog's chin and continued walking toward the house.

A soft glow of light from the windows shone golden onto the patio.

Sarah's stomach rumbled and growled. The welcoming scent of saffron, rice and chicken hung heavy in the still air of the courtyard as they stepped up to the patio.

An older woman opened the door for them. She wore a black abaya as was proper for the mixed company of family and foreigners. Abdullah introduced her as his mother, Samara. She welcomed each of the visitors graciously in Arabic as they entered.

Sarah stepped inside to see three teenage boys and a young woman watching her. Their curious looks were amusing after Gino's line of questioning on the ride in.

The entry room was small and seemed to be the traditional room for entertaining with low, upholstered benches lining every wall. Though it was small, Sarah estimated they could probably fit about twenty people comfortably. They most likely had family meetings or audiences in this room.

Samara led them into a large dining room devoid of furniture where the floor had been dressed with a tablecloth and a small feast had been laid out. A huge platter of saffron rice served as the centerpiece, surrounded by platters of grilled meats, meats in sauces, crusty flatbread, vegetables, and fresh fruit off the tree.

Sarah tried to ignore the sound of her stomach and hoped that nobody else heard it, until Brian eyed her and gave her a playful wink. Apparently, he heard it over the chitchat of the women and teens.

Hamza said something quietly to Brian and then Brian turned to Sarah. "Generally the women and men eat separately when entertaining but because I've filled them in on you and we need to discuss the plan with all of them, the women will be eating in here with the men tonight."

Sarah nodded, aware of the cultural allowances they would be making, and whispered back to Brian. "I don't care where I eat so long as I do it soon. I'm starving."

Abdullah, the head of the household, introduced the entourage to his sister, Bashira, and his three much younger brothers.

They all seemed more than a little surprised and somewhat pleased when Sarah addressed them in Arabic. She could see why her language skills had been a big plus in her selection for her job with the C.I.A. Her Russian and Arabic had certainly been coming in handy as of late.

Even in an abaya, Bashira was a beauty with flawless olive skin and unadorned almond eyes. Probably only in her twenties, there was something of the slave about her. The bruise on her cheek was a dead giveaway.

In her years as a cop, Sarah had seen women who had been abused and that was the same look she saw in Bashira's soft brown eyes. Her heart went out to the poor young woman who had been born into a hard life that was probably made harder by mistreatment.

Sarah respected the traditions of the land and spoke only when spoken to at dinner. When the women rose to clear the empty dishes, she rose to help as well.

Bashira insisted she remain seated.

Coffee was served and the men took out cigarettes as the women returned and sat quietly.

Sarah looked questioningly to Brian. She didn't want to offend her hosts and knew the Arabs, especially the rural people, took male and female roles very seriously. She knew quitting smoking would be a good thing for her, but not here and not now.

He nodded, indicating it was all right to blaze up if she wanted to.

With some relief, she pulled her cigarette case from a cargo pocket and took one out. She remembered the custom from her military assignment in Turkey and passed the cigarettes around as a courtesy. They all took one. The younger boys seemed especially impressed.

Hamza took much interest in the gold case engraved with delicate scrollwork. When Sarah offered it as a gift, he protested but she insisted and he seemed quite pleased with the expensive trinket.

As they sipped their coffee and smoked Sarah's cigarettes, they discussed their plan to destroy Nikolai. Samara and Bashira sat quietly in a corner and listened.

Abdullah spoke first. "I take no pleasure in watching you go to that place after what my sister has suffered at the hands of Nikolai's man."

Sarah looked at Bashira. "May I ask what happened?"

Bashira's eyes glistened with the threat of tears, and she looked down at her knees.

Abdullah spoke for her. "The worst thing a man can do to a respectable girl. She has been soiled. No man will have her now. She cannot marry."

Sarah took a deep breath and swallowed back the rage building inside over the rape of an innocent. She bent her head and covered her face with her hands for a moment as she composed herself. She gazed at Bashira, who held her head down in what must certainly have been shame. "I am so sorry. Bashira, I promise you will never have to go back there again."

Bashira looked up at Sarah, eyes wet with uncried tears. A simple nod was all they needed between them.

"But what can you do that she couldn't?" Samara's loud and anxious voice surprised Sarah.

Sarah smiled at the older woman and without words she reached under her abaya to produce the SIG forty-fives.

Bashira gasped. "*Muharib.*" She slapped her hand over her mouth.

Sarah understood the whispered word meaning 'warrior.' She smiled at Bashira and nodded.

She laid the handguns on the floor in front of her and reached under the abaya again to retrieve a stainless steel throwing knife from the scabbard tied around her leg.

The men passed the SIGs around, admiring them and speaking the international language of men who respect firearms. Then they passed around the knife. Muhammad, who apparently questioned the ability to do damage with such a small knife, ran his finger over the blade and cut himself. A surprised grunt escaped his lips and his brows furrowed as he stared at Sarah, probably unsure what to make of the bold American woman who knew their language and customs and promised payback for his kinswoman's rape.

Brian assured the men Sarah knew full well how to use the weapons. They nodded approvingly.

Once the weapons made their way back to her, Sarah holstered the SIGs, wiped the blade with her abaya and tucked the knife back into the scabbard.

The looks of admiration from Bashira and Samara were unmistakable.

Muhammad yawned and Hamza nodded to Brian. "It is late and the women have work to do in the morning." The men stood and Sarah followed suit.

Brian gave Sarah a hug. "Watch your ass in there. They've probably roughed Vince up. Just remember he's a tough S.O.B. and don't let that temper get the best of you."

Sarah bit her bottom lip and breathed deep. "We can do this." It had been easier to think about the plan and prepare for battle than to think about what Vince might look like when she got there.

Brian released her from the hug and his eyes sparkled. "We can do this." He glanced around the room, seemingly making a head count, then turned to Sarah. "Okay, we'll drop Gino off at his quarters and then Hamza, Abdullah, Muhammad, and I will stay at the Bedouin camp with the rest of the guys. You'll walk to Nikolai's with Samara in the morning. Jason will pick you up tomorrow night as planned, as soon as you leave Nikolai's compound. Got the camera?"

Sarah patted her front pocket through the abaya and nodded.

"And no chatting with Chris while you're inside the house. Too risky."

Sarah tapped her ear. "I know. Radio silence. No worries."

Hamza, Abdulla and Muhammad each gave Sarah a deferential nod before leaving.

After the men drove off, Bashira and Samara showed Sarah to the room they shared. The room was Spartan with a full sized bed being its only furniture. The three of them were crowded in the bed together. Sarah was too exhausted to mind. She had a belly full of good food and would see Vince tomorrow. She fell asleep as soon as her head hit the pillow.

Twenty-Eight

A light hand shook Sarah's arm. Groggy after a night of terrible dreams, she looked to the window. It was still dark outside, but Samara assured her it was morning and time to go to work.

Butterflies burst into action in Sarah's stomach.

Today I'll finally see Vince. Today!

Sarah jumped out of bed, ready to finally take action.

Samara left the room, but Bashira sat up in the bed and quietly watched Sarah prepare.

She slipped on her boots, laced them and stuck the Ka-Bar knife in its hidden scabbard. She pulled the two small nylon knife cases from her duffel bag and strapped one onto each calf. She pulled one of the shiny, stainless steel kunai knives out, held it up to the light and smiled at Bashira.

Bashira returned the smile.

Sarah picked up one of the SIGs, ejected the ammunition magazine, locked it in the open position, and eyed the barrel to be sure it was clear. She smiled, pulled the trigger, and slapped the magazine back in before holstering the loaded weapon. She did the same with the second handgun. She plucked two more ammunition magazines from her bag, checked to be sure they were full, and tucked them into a front pocket of the cargo pants under her abaya. She hoped she wouldn't need the weapons today but felt more secure knowing she had them.

She walked out into the kitchen where Samara had made coffee.

She handed Sarah a small cup of the strong brew and then handed her a plate of bread and fruit left over from the night before.

Sarah thanked her and ate quickly. Her hands were shaking with excitement about finding Vince. She couldn't get there soon enough.

Samara placed a calming hand over Sarah's. "He is well. They have him in a bedroom upstairs. He is comfortable."

Reassured by Samara's calm voice, Sarah smiled a grateful smile. "Yes, but for how long?"

"They will not kill him yet. They think he will choose to do business with them. What you do need to worry about is the big Australian." A shadow came over Samara's face. "He is a terrible and cruel man. He will be rough. Be careful."

Bashira entered the small kitchen as Samara spoke.

Sarah saw the desperate look on Bashira's face and anger rose hot and hateful inside her. There were many things that could be forgiven, but rape would never be one. "He'll pay for what he's done. I promise you that."

"It is time to go." Samara stood and prepared to leave.

Sarah flashed Bashira a smile and gulped down the last of her coffee.

No matter what her mission might be, when Sarah was on the job, she always knew Chris had her back…well at least in a technological sense. Sarah wore a tiny earpiece the size of a pencil eraser that enabled her to communicate with Chris. She never went into an operation without making sure Chris was with her. "Chris, can you hear me?"

Chris cleared his throat. "Loud and clear, sweetheart. Good morning!"

Sarah rolled her eyes. "I woke you up again, didn't I?"

"I consider myself one of the honored few."

She smiled at the compliment. "Flatterer. Hopefully we find Vince today. Samara said they're keeping him in a bedroom upstairs."

"Good luck. Call when you get a fix or if you need the cavalry. We're standing by."

"Thanks. I will."

~~~

They saw Nikolai's compound long before they came near it. High concrete walls kept the desert from swallowing it up. They walked nearly a mile before they reached the large wooden gate Sarah had seen in the satellite photos.

Sarah examined the ten-foot concrete wall of the compound as she walked through the gate. She kept her head down in an attempt to avoid raising any suspicions in the sleepy looking man posted at the gate. The wall was at least two feet thick, and the house was probably twenty yards away from the gate, providing a nice clear zone in case anyone tried to blow the wall or the gate open.

Nikolai may be bad but he's no dummy.

All was silent within the walls of the compound.

Samara explained their job. "I make breakfast while Bashira cleans the common rooms in the morning. We have one hour before Nikolai and his men wake up.

Sarah took advantage of the time she had to take pictures of everything—walls, windows, gates, doors, hallways. She didn't go anywhere without taking pictures. It would make things easier if she could just email the pictures directly to Chris, but Sarah wasn't the least bit surprised when she didn't get a signal on her cell phone.

They don't call it the Empty Quarter for nothing.

She systematically mapped the lower level of the house with photos because she knew it would help when they took the compound. After she returned to the Bedouin camp, Chris would download the photos and create a virtual map and 3D image for the guys to plan the attack.

Her feet itched with the need to get upstairs and make contact with Vince, but Samara told her the second floor was off limits until Nikolai came downstairs.

Samara reassured Sarah. "We brought your man breakfast, lunch and dinner yesterday. He'll be fine today."

A resigned sigh escaped Sarah's lips.

The last thing she wanted to do was draw attention to herself by going upstairs when she shouldn't be there. It would be easier to locate him while everyone else was downstairs anyway.

Twenty-Nine

It seemed like forever but Nikolai and his men finally came down to the main floor. The first man down the stairs was well over six feet and two hundred fifty pounds. Another followed closely behind him. He stood just a hint over six feet and looked to be about two hundred pounds. The two men busied themselves with a large breakfast laid out in the kitchen by Samara while Sarah took a tray to Nikolai in his office.

He didn't look up from his computer. "You're late, girl."

Sarah held back the urge to speak, to spit in Nikolai's face and hold a forty-five to his head until he produced Vince.

It would be so easy. I could do it right now and nobody would give a damn.

The tactical Sarah won out. She kept her eyes down and walked tentatively like she had watched Bashira do in her home.

Calm down. We need to destroy this place and send a message. The last thing we need is to be hunted by the Russian mob for the rest of our lives.

Nikolai dismissed her as soon as she'd poured his coffee.

She left the room as quickly as she could and made her way upstairs, snapping pictures all the way. She made the beds as instructed but didn't clean a thing.

The only thing I'm cleaning here is Nikolai's clock!

Panic grabbed her by the neck and squeezed as she searched every room for Vince, but he was nowhere to be found. Her heart raced.

Breathe deep, Sarah. You don't need to be one of those stupid movie chicks who gets nervous and stupid. Get a frickin' grip.

She returned to the kitchen, careful to avoid the two thugs who were on their way out. The big one grabbed her ass as she walked, but she ignored him and walked a little faster to escape his grip.

Behind her and in an Australian accent, she heard one of the men speak. "Yeah, mate. She wants it again. When we finish with this Hennessee guy, I'm gonna fix her up." They both chuckled as they walked away.

Sarah half smiled to herself.

Somebody's gonna get fixed up all right. I'm gonna fix you up good, you son of a bitch.

Samara looked up from the dishes with panic in her eyes. "Don't let him close to you."

"He's the one?"

Samara's eyes welled with tears as she nodded.

Sarah locked that information away for later when she could use it and focused on the matter at hand. "Samara, he's not upstairs."

Samara looked back down at the dishes she was washing. "Then they've put him back in the cell."

"The *cell*?"

"Yes, downstairs. The small storage room."

"Was that where the men were going?"

"No, they are going to the village. They will be back soon, but you have time to check if you go now." She pointed Sarah to a door off the kitchen that led downstairs.

Sarah's feet barely touched the stairs, her steps quick and silent. It was a good ten degrees cooler in the basement. She snapped pictures every few feet but the lighting was poor, and she didn't want to explain a flash if anyone was down there. She opened the first door she came to. It was a large windowless room with a table and a few chairs but nothing else. The next door she came to was locked. She said a silent prayer for Vince. It was answered when she heard a shuffle inside.

She leaned close to the door and hoped she wasn't about to blow her cover by whispering into it. "Vince?"

"Sarah?" The voice was ragged but it was Vince.

Her skin went cold with relief and she placed the palms of her hands against the door to be just a few inches closer to him. "Thank God you're alive!"

She heard footsteps behind the door. "Sarah, did they catch you?" His voice came from only inches away this time.

Sarah smiled. "No. I'm here to take you home."

"Are the guys with you?"

Sarah heard a noise at the top of the stairs. "Shh…"

The Australian was clomping down the stairs. "He might be a little more willing to talk if we soften him up first."

106

The guy thumping along behind him just chuckled.

Sarah hurried to the other end of the hall and ducked into a utility room containing the central air conditioner, an oil furnace, a large generator and two large water heaters. She swore silently as she strained to hear over the sound of the machinery. She cracked the door open and watched as the two men dragged a bound Vince out of the storage room and shoved him into the large, windowless room perfectly set up for interrogation.

Nothing like a crappy chair and a lack of daylight to really throw a body off their game.

Sarah knew she would have to walk by the room in order to get back up to the kitchen. She breathed deeply and steeled herself for what she knew she'd see.

~~~

Vince sat still as the smaller guy tied his hands behind him in the chair and Ian, the big Australian, taunted him with the possibility of another strike to the face with the butt of his rifle.

Was it Sarah? Was I dreaming?

Vince's heart pumped double-time with excitement.

It was Sarah. They're finally here. Too bad Nikolai was wise to my stalling. I might have been able to wait it out in comfort.

Vince's mind shot back to reality when a massive fist hit him like a rocket in the side of his face. "*Fuck!*"

Ian laughed. "You're fucked all right, mate." He hit Vince again just for good measure.

Pain shot down his jaw and into his neck as his head swung to the left at light speed. He could taste warm, sweet blood and spit a mouthful of it on the Aussie's pants, smiling at his handiwork.

Ian glared. "You think that's funny?"

"Yeah, I do." Vince grinned even though he could feel his own blood streaming down his chin.

"Oh, that's a real belly laugh, ain't it?"

Vince saw it coming and tensed his abdominal muscles before the fist made contact. He grunted with the force of the punch.

"Hey, girl. Come in here."

When his vision cleared, Vince looked up to see the Arab girl at the door.

The Aussie had stopped her as she was walking by.

Her head was down as it always was. No doubt she thought she'd get a beating too.

Vince, well aware of his own situation, yearned to do something, anything, to help Bashira. He'd done plenty of bad things in his life, but the three things he couldn't stomach were beating women, children, or dogs.

Sarah had been there. He was sure of it. *If only she'd storm in, guns-a-blazing and save the poor girl from this bastard's abuse.*

Ian motioned toward Bashira. "Come here, little girl. I've got something *big* for you."

"Come on, Ian. Let's just finish him up and go."

It was the first time Vince had heard the other guy do anything but chuckle.

Ian leered at Bashira. "We've got plenty of time. You want to go first?"

Chuckles shook his head. "Na, Ian, I don't want any part of that."

"Suit yourself." Ian bellowed at the girl. "Get your ass over here, girl!"

Jesus, he's gonna rape her right here. Fucking sadistic bastard.

Bashira crept slowly toward Ian. Her hands were tucked into her abaya as if she were trying to hide under the fabric. Her head was still bowed and Vince was grateful he couldn't see her face.

She's probably scared shitless and there isn't a thing I can do to help her. Or is there?

"Hey, you stupid pig. Is that all you got? A couple punches are all you've got in ya, huh? Probably can't even hang in a bar fight, can you?"

This time, Vince didn't see the boot coming until it was too late. He heard a rib crack and flew backwards with the chair. He winced in pain as his head hit the hard concrete floor. He closed his eyes and took a few seconds to breathe. Relief washed over the pain when he realized the rib hadn't punctured a lung.

Bashira is still in the room. Got to get the girl out.

Vince looked up and took a deep breath as he eyed the Aussie who was about to grab Bashira. "You kick like a girl."

"Are you that stupid? Do you really want me to kill you now?"

"I don't care what the fuck you do, you big fucking Nancy but this ain't no spectator sport. Get that girl out of here."

"Get the hell out of here and make me some coffee, bitch." Ian pushed Bashira toward the door and she stumbled.

Something strange about her registered in Vince's mind.

Combat boots? Why is a poor Saudi girl wearing top of the line, lightweight combat boots?

Before he could work out the thought in his head, a truck that looked an awful lot like a fist hit him and everything went black.

Thirty

The Aussie and his sidekick locked Vince in the storage room shortly after Sarah left the torture chamber. She watched through the kitchen window as they hopped into one of the SUVs out in the yard and drove out the gate.

Sarah snuck back down to the basement and tried to talk to Vince again, but he was either asleep or unconscious. She listened at the door to hear him breathing and took small comfort in that.

If he were dead, they'd have dumped the body on their way into town.

Sarah walked around the house with a dust cloth and a camera most of the morning. Nikolai had almost caught her once but she stuffed the tiny camera in the cloth and scurried out of the room before he could speak to her.

When the Aussie and his flunky returned from their trip, Sarah stayed near Samara and did so for the rest of the day. It would completely compromise the mission if she had to kill somebody today. She couldn't risk Vince's life or Samara's.

While Samara fixed dinner, Sarah kept a low profile doing laundry, scrubbing floors and thinking about the many ways she could make that Australian bastard pay for his expanding list of crimes.

When Nikolai had finished his dinner and the dishes were cleared and cleaned, Samara looked at Sarah with kind, aged eyes. "Do you have what you need?"

Everything but Vince.

Sarah despaired that the day might never end. "Yes. Can we go now?"

Samara nodded and seemed relieved as well.

Once they walked out of the compound and were out of earshot of the guard inside the gate, Sarah called Chris. "We're on our way back now. Send somebody to pick me up."

"Already ahead of you. Jason should be pulling up at your location any second now."

Sarah's mood lightened and she smiled as she looked up into an empty blue sky. "Christopher, did you Lojack me?"

"Girl, please. You know better than that. Lojack doesn't have the juice to track you, but yeah, I've been following your signature. Can't let anything happen to my best girl. Did you find Vince?"

"And *you* know better than to ask a question like that. Of course, I did."

"What's his status?"

"Alive." Nothing more needed to be said. Sarah knew Chris would understand her simple answer and resolute tone and not ask for more details right now.

~~~

Jason hadn't even stopped the truck before Sarah jumped out and jogged into the tent. A cool wave of relief washed over her. She could be herself here instead of playing the helpless Arab girl. She pulled the abaya off and flung it onto the floor of the tent as soon as she ran in. She pulled the phone out of her pocket and took it directly to Chris so he could download the photos and start mapping the interior of Nikolai's compound.

Will was walking across the camp when Jason drove up and appeared by her side in seconds. Always cool, he sat beside her on the carpeted floor as she lit the cigarette she'd been dying for all day. Jason and Brian came in and sat in the corner with them.

She took a long drag of her cigarette, savored it as she collected her thoughts, and then started downloading the situation report. "They're keeping him in a small cell in the basement. Today was the first day they worked him over. I'm pretty sure I heard a rib crack so he's going to need medical attention. Other than that, he's gonna be pretty banged up."

Will rested a hand on her shoulder. "You saw them beating him?"

Sarah took a long drag and nodded. Frustration knotted her stomach. "There was nothing I could do without compromising all of us and putting him in more danger." Tears pushed for release and she blinked hard. It wasn't a hopeless sadness bringing the tears. It was anger and frustration at not being able to stop the abuse inflicted on Vince. She was engulfed by a wave of damning thoughts.

I just watched. I didn't stop it from happening.

Will interrupted her moment of self-condemnation. "You did the right thing, Sarah. You're right. It would have been a clusterfuck if you'd done anything to stop them."

Sarah looked up into Will's baby blue, empathetic eyes. She rubbed her face, wishing the memory to go away. "I know, but I felt every hit as if it were me."

He put his arm around her and pulled her close. "I know, Sarah, but he's a tough nut. He'll get through this. We just need to make sure we have all the information we need. Did you get pictures?"

Sarah took a deep breath, closed her eyes, and balled her fists a few times to get a grip on her thoughts.

That's enough of the pity party bullshit, Sarah.

Chris spoke as he continued tapping away at his computer. "Yeah, I'm putting it all together here." He looked up at Sarah. "Check this out and make sure I've got it right."

Sarah moved closer to Chris so she could see his computer screen.

He'd done some 3D imaging magic and reproduced the entire house and compound in virtually no time at all.

Once Sarah confirmed that Chris had it all correct, Will examined every foot of the compound and made notes on his legal pad.

No more than an hour after Sarah had arrived, Will began briefing the assembled crew on when and how they'd attack the compound. A contingency plan was set in case Vince was in mortal danger, but, if he could last the day, the whole thing would go down at sunset the following evening.

Thirty-One

Her second morning in Nikolai's house and her anxiety was eating at her from the inside out. Sarah huffed as she picked up the pitcher of water and placed it on the tray.

Samara nodded to her. "Patience."

Sarah took a deep breath and steeled herself. She'd see Vince soon. *He is still alive.*

Sarah stopped outside the heavy wooden door of the interrogation room. The sound of someone inside being beaten made her ache.

Oh, God, make it stop.

She knocked on the door a little more forcefully than she should have. Wishing the banging on the door would make the beating stop.

"Get in here!" The door flew open and the large man with the Australian accent and blood on his shirt gave her an evil grin that made her skin crawl.

What else has he done to that poor girl? Bashira was so happy to not have to come here.

Sarah lowered her eyes and quickly entered the room, placing the tray on the table off to the right.

Vince's breaths came in heavy rasps. She looked up and saw what she had hoped she would never see. Vince was bound to a chair. His head and face were bloody, bruised and swollen. His shirt was nothing but rags held together by a few threads.

Sarah's blood boiled. Her face grew hot and her need to rip somebody open with her bare hands grew with every gasp from Vince's lungs.

I swear I'll make them pay for this.

After a few beats of her heart that seemed like forever, Vince looked up at her.

She suspected he wouldn't recognize her. Changing her eye color from green to brown and her much darker skin color would throw anyone off.

Vince took several deep breaths as he studied her face.

Sarah felt two hands grip her shoulders. "Thank you, Bashira. I could use a little break from this work."

A break? How's about I break your arm, you son of a bitch?

Sarah tried to demure from his grip but he held tight.

"Why don't we go back to my room and you can wash this blood off me."

Oh, yeah, you're a smooth one, aren't you?

Sarah dropped a glass as a pretense to get away from his iron grip. She tried to kneel to pick it up.

"Clumsy, bitch. Leave it! I said I want to take a break." He threw Sarah against the table, and she suddenly knew exactly what he had done to Bashira. The reason her family wanted Nikolai and his people gone was all too clear when Sarah felt the Australian's hard shaft against her buttocks.

The fire of rage inside her burned furiously. Options ripped through her mind as he fumbled with his belt. There was a Ka-Bar knife in her boot and several on her legs. It would take little effort to reach one and castrate the rapist standing behind her. The forty-fives were just a few inches from her sweating palms. She could blow this bastard's head off in two seconds flat. But how would she and Vince get out? The compound was crawling with people today. She'd seen, from the kitchen windows, hired guns, and muscle loading and unloading trucks inside the compound walls.

Sarah knew she had to stay calm. She had to find a way to put this guy off. She had to find a way to make Vince understand that they were here to free him.

The bile that burned in Sarah's stomach gave her the edge she needed. She started coughing as hard as she could. When she put her hand over her mouth, she forced a finger so deep into her throat that breakfast had to heed the call. The coughing caught the Aussie off guard and he stepped back. Sarah took the opening and turned as though to fall into his arms just as a stinking mess of hummus, feta and olives flew from her mouth. His boots were covered in an instant.

Yes!

Sarah's head flew back with force as a huge hand flew at her from the left.

She stumbled and fell to the hummus, feta and olive covered floor, and she was never so happy to be sitting in a pool of her own vomit. Her head was splitting. The Aussie had really smacked her hard, and she saw stars intermingled with the vomit. She stole a sideways glance at Vince.

He was watching closely with a look of concern on his face.

Sarah winked.

Vince's swollen eyes opened as wide as the swelling allowed.

Sarah thought she saw recognition in his face but she wasn't sure. Cold fear grabbed her.

Oh, please recognize me, Vince. Please?

She had one last hope. She bit her bottom lip, lifted her eyebrows, and gave him an evil grin.

The Aussie kicked at her but she dodged his filthy, puke-covered boot.

"You disgusting cunt! Look at my boots! Clean this up now!"

Sarah nodded and gave a few extra coughs just for show as she scrambled from the room for towels.

When she ran into the kitchen, Samara gasped. "What has he done to you?"

Sarah rinsed her mouth quickly in the sink. "It wasn't what he did, it was what he *tried* to do."

"But how did you…?"

She spit a mouthful of water into the sink. "I threw up on him."

Samara gasped.

"Don't you worry, Samara." Sarah whispered. "I'll make that bastard pay for what he did to Bashira."

Samara covered her mouth in horror. "No. He will kill you."

Sarah rinsed her hands and wiped them with a clean towel. She turned to face the poor old woman who had no doubt seen and heard her daughter being abused by this monster and could do nothing but stand by helplessly. Pity for Bashira's mother filled her heart.

"Not before *I* kill *him*."

As Sarah picked up a large bowl to take downstairs, she noticed something crawling in the sand outside the kitchen door. She grabbed the towel and ran outside in time to scoop up a small, golden-colored scorpion. She scampered back inside, tossed it into the bowl and covered it with the towel, hoping she'd have a chance to use the little demon.

It probably won't kill him but a sting or two would be good for him.

She smiled at Samara and made her way back downstairs.

As she approached the open door of the interrogation room, she heard the Australian rattling off curse words as fast as he could.

Sarah looked only at Vince as she hurried into the room.

Yes, he knows it's me. He knows!

She knelt near the puddle of vomit to start wiping it up.

The Australian had removed his boots and left them near the puddle, cursing at her between sips of water. "Get that shit off my boots, bitch. When I'm done with this guy, I'm gonna take care of you once and for all."

She kept her back to him while she worked quickly. Carefully, she grabbed the scorpion with the towel and dropped it into a boot before wiping them both clean.

It would be worth the beating and if it came to it, she'd slice the fucker's throat, plan be damned, and break Vince out right now.

She carried the boots over to where the Australian sat drinking a glass of water, and knelt before him.

He grinned and gave a self-satisfied laugh. "Now that's more like it." He lifted a foot for Sarah to put on his boot. "It's about time you see who the master is here."

Sarah nodded dutifully, eyes down the whole time. She slipped the boot on the stinking foot he offered and laced it up. Then she loosened the laces of the other boot, while stealing a glance at Vince who seemed to be watching, spellbound.

The Australian offered his other foot and Sarah slid the boot onto it, pulling the laces tight as quickly as possible to lock the desert demon inside.

The Australian bellowed in pain as he kicked wildly from his seat. "What the fuck have you done! Did you put a razor blade in there?"

Sarah backed up, out of kicking range while the man yanked at his boot, cursing the whole time.

He flung the boot aside to reveal the little golden scorpion, still alive and hacking at the man's foot for dear life.

116

Sarah tried to appear shocked while glee bubbled up inside her.

With every sting, the Australian screamed louder. Sweat formed on the Aussie's face as Sarah saw the poison take effect. She knew a Middle Eastern scorpion this size wouldn't kill a healthy adult, but it should make him good and sick.

The Aussie started gasping for breath and holding his chest. He wheezed as though his airway was closing.

Allah be praised. Anaphylactic shock! Who knew he'd be allergic to it?

Sarah looked into his eyes and saw them dilate. He tried to stand but fell to the floor, slippery with Sarah's breakfast, gripping his chest.

Sarah rolled him over and looked into his eyes as a layer of fog formed over them. She spoke in English. "Somebody's been waiting for you. Are you ready to answer for what you've done?"

A tiny gasp of surprise escaped his lips before his body went limp and the breathing stopped.

Sarah looked at the scorpion, still attacking the man's now swollen foot.

She grabbed the Aussie's discarded boot and crushed the small arachnid. Then she calmly stood, closed the door of the room, and poured a glass of water. She took the water to Vince and held it for him to drink.

His voice was rough and raspy when he spoke. "You're a cruel bitch but I love you. What took you so long?"

Sarah shook her head and smiled with the joy of knowing the experience hadn't killed his sense of humor. "I couldn't decide what to wear."

Vince started to laugh but winced and groaned from the pain of the newly broken rib.

"Why has he been torturing you?"

"Nikolai made me an offer, and I refused." He fixed his swollen eyes on her. "You know you have to sell this now, right?"

"Yeah, I know. Just drink a little more water first."

Vince guzzled the rest of the water. "When are you busting me out?"

"Tonight, when the staff leaves." She kissed him gently on the only part of his head that didn't seem to be bumped or bruised. "I love you."

Sarah quietly opened the door to the room and looked down the hallway.

Nobody there.

She threw the glass to the floor and screamed in terror like she had never screamed before.

Samara came running down the stairs, abaya flowing with the speed of her descent.

Two men followed her.

When the men saw the huge, strapping Aussie on the floor they raced to see what had happened. One of them looked for a pulse then shook his head at the second guy. He shrugged. "No big loss. He was a sick bastard anyway."

The second guy spoke to Samara as he pulled a phone from his pocket. "What happened?"

Sarah acted hysterical and rattled off what had happened in Arabic. "*Oh, Mama! Oh, mama! I was cleaning the floor and heard him fall. I tried to help him but there was nothing I could do. I couldn't help him!*" Sarah wailed and sobbed. "*It was a scorpion. By the time I'd killed it, it was too late.*" She added more horrific wailing as she clung to the hem of Samara's abaya.

"There, there, child. You poor thing." Samara helped her up. She looked at the man who'd asked her what happened. "A scorpion. Some people are allergic to them. I'll take my daughter back to the kitchen to compose herself." She helped Sarah out of the room and back to the kitchen where she started cleaning up Sarah's abaya.

Sarah leaned against the sink on her elbows and bowed her head in relief. Nikolai's dungeon master would no longer cause pain for Vince, and he would never commit another act of cruelty upon a woman. Gratitude for the timeliness of a scurrying scorpion filled her heart. She knew somehow, God or not, the universe had taken care of things. She stood, took Samara's hands in hers, and held them as she looked into the woman's eyes. "Your daughter can rest easy now."

Tears filled Samara's eyes, but there were no words.

Sarah didn't need any. She understood.

~~~

Nikolai's voice came booming from the hallway. "Samara! Samara!"

Samara ran toward the voice as Sarah finished cleaning up.

When Samara returned, she handed Sarah a bundle of clothes and spoke briefly. "Mr. Hennessee is being taken back to his room upstairs. The master wants fresh clothes brought to him there." A silver colored key flashed in the palm of Samara's hand. "Here."

Sarah grabbed the key like a lifeline. "Thank you, Samara."

Sarah took the back stairs up to Vince's room. She waited around the corner until she heard the men lock the door.

There was a thump that sounded like someone being pushed into a wall and one of the men sounded indignant. "What?"

"Somebody's gotta stay. You gonna stay and watch him?"

"What for? He's in no condition to bust out. He'll keep until morning."

She waited as the men walked downstairs. Sarah slipped quietly around the corner, unlocked the door, and let herself in.

Vince was lying on the bed, battered and bloody, but his chest rose and fell with quiet breaths.

Her body threatened to collapse with relief, but she reminded herself to stay strong. They weren't out of the woods yet.

He turned his head and gave Sarah a swollen smile. "Baby, you really are a sight for sore eyes."

Sarah hurried to the bathroom for a wet washcloth. "I'm so sorry we took so long to get here." She rushed to the bed and started cleaning the cuts on his face.

"This ain't nothin'. I'll be back to my old self in no time." He sat up with a quiet grunt, took the cool washcloth from her hand, and put it over a swollen eye. "That's nice." He focused his good eye on her. "What's the plan?"

"We've got a camp set up a couple clicks to the west. Chris and two security guys are staying there. Jason, Guinea and four others are coming in on the Blackhawk with some hellfire."

"Guinea? Guinea's here?"

"Yeah." Sarah nodded. "We've got two trucks that will each transport six guys. Will and Brian are coming in with them."

"Okay, when is kickoff?"

"Sunset. Samara will pretend to be sick and leave early so we're clear of non-combatants. It's a liquidation sale."

"Good."

Sarah went back to the bathroom for a fresh washcloth and the clothes she'd left there. "Here, put these on." She pulled a SIG and an extra magazine of ammunition from under her abaya and dropped them on the bed as Vince dressed. "Keep these close."

"Ahh." Vince sighed as he picked up the gun and tucked it in the waistband of the pants he'd just stepped into. "You kill with scorpions and bring me my favorite handgun. I'm never getting rid of you."

She raised an eyebrow and winked. "Good luck trying."

He winced as he slipped the shirt on. "What's the extract plan?"

"We'll clean up and retreat back to the camp. Brian's cousins will get rid of the trucks."

"Wait...Brian's *cousins?*"

"I don't have time to explain. Just try to keep up, okay?" Sarah continued. "Brian will take the guys to the airport in the civilian chopper. Jason will take you, me, Will, Guinea and Chris back to the island in the Blackhawk. If we lose a chopper, there is a cave one-point-three clicks south of the camp. We'll fallback to that position and Leo will pick us up at oh-three-hundred. Got it?"

"Yeah. Good plan. But who are all the extra guys?"

Sarah took an exasperated breath. She knew Vince was hurting and information would make him feel better, but she couldn't risk getting caught in his room. "Leo is a buddy of Will's. The rest are contractors. Hopefully there won't be a fight but, if there is, we wanted to be ready."

"Leave it to Will to cover all the bases."

"I'd better get out of here. The whole house is still in an uproar over that Aussie dick. I'll be back to bust you out in five hours and ten minutes. Get some sleep. It's gonna be a long night."

Sarah bent to kiss him on the lips.

Vince grabbed her wrist. "Sarah." His swollen face appeared a little more serious than it had a moment ago.

She frowned at Vince. "Baby, I gotta get my ass out of here."

He nodded. "Whatever happens tonight, I love you."

A tingle of happiness raced up the back of her neck. "I love you too." She grinned. "But there's no *'whatever'* when Will plans an operation. We're getting you out of here tonight."

Thirty-Two

Samara seemed shaken when Sarah returned to the kitchen after spending several hours quietly dusting and memorizing every inch of the mansion. "Sarah, the men are staying tonight."

"What do you mean?" Sarah looked out the kitchen window to see eight men milling about the trucks that they were supposed to have loaded and moved before sunset.

"Nikolai is having them stay so they can all leave with him first thing in the morning." A shadow rolled over her face. "Nikolai isn't planning to take Vince with him."

Sarah's heart raced as she realized what would happen.

That bastard is just going to kill Vince and dump him in the desert.

"When is Nikolai planning to kill him?"

"Tonight."

"Did they say *when*?"

"I couldn't hear them."

Several men walked into the kitchen and sat down at the large table.

Samara busied herself with a pot of chai and several plates of cheese and fruits. It was clearly break time for the men, and there was no way Sarah could get upstairs to warn Vince.

Samara continued serving the men their tea. When all the men had been served, Samara prepared a tray and instructed Sarah that it was time for Nikolai's tea.

Oh, my God! I'm serving frigging tea to these people when I should be warning Vince and Chris. Fuckity-fuck-fuck-fuck!

Sarah took the tea tray to Nikolai's study and served in silence.

Nikolai glanced up at her.

She turned away quickly and busied herself with some dishes on the tray until he went back to his computer. When his attention was engaged elsewhere, Sarah served his cake and left quickly.

By the time she returned to the kitchen, the men had finished their tea and several of them were making their way upstairs.

"Where are they going?"

"They're going to the guest rooms to sleep until it is time to leave. The others are closing up the outbuildings and then they'll be napping too."

Sarah reached into the hidden pocket of her abaya that allowed her to touch the loaded .45 strapped to her thigh. "Then we wait."

~~~

Sarah looked outside. The sun was nearly down and the guys would be here soon. She had to get Samara out of the line of fire. "Samara, you should get going now."

Samara grabbed Sarah's hands, panic lit her eyes. "Will you be all right?"

Sarah squeezed Samara's hands. "Yes, of course. You should go."

"I can't thank you enough for what you've done."

Sarah grabbed her by the shoulders and turned her toward the door. "Just go now and stay safe. Please?"

The last of the men returned as Samara left. One of them looked at Sarah. "Where is *she* going?"

Sarah responded quietly just in case they might have known Bashira's voice. "My mother is old and unwell. She is upset by what happened earlier. It has been a difficult day for her so I will finish up for her."

"You'd better get to work on dinner. We'll all be hungry when we wake up and we have things to do tonight."

"Yes, sir." Sarah nodded and turned to start measuring rice so she'd look like she was working. She knew full well that nobody in this house would be eating dinner tonight.

Soon.

Sarah listened for the sound of a helicopter but there was only silence. She looked out the window toward the last burning embers of the sun.

Soon.

When the men finally left the kitchen and she heard doors close upstairs, she made her way up the creaky kitchen stairs.

She reached inside her abaya and pulled the warm key from within her bra. She listened for signs of anyone awake.

Silence.

She was suddenly aware of even the smallest noise as she listened for the helicopter.

Still no sound.

The key slid into the lock and she nearly jumped as the latch clicked open. She put a finger to her lips as she opened the door.

Of course, he knows to be quiet, you idiot.

She dropped her hand as she peeked in and saw Vince standing by the door in the fresh clothes she'd brought him earlier.

She gasped at the sight of him. The swelling hadn't gone down, and the bruises had darkened on his face. White-hot rage burned inside her at what Nikolai had done to him. "It's time."

The bruises and broken rib didn't slow him down. When it was time for action, he was ready to roll as always.

"Let's do it. Where's Nikolai?"

"He's still in the study."

"Good." Vince pulled the forty-five from under his shirt and grabbed Sarah with his free hand. "Let's put an end to that bastard now."

They hurried down the stairs and were both thrown against the wall of the stairway as an explosion rocked the compound. Vince jumped the rest of the stairs and Sarah followed.

One of the trucks parked outside was engulfed in flames.

Another explosion rocked the compound and then another as a massive hole appeared in the concrete wall outside.

Men came running down the stairs behind Vince and Sarah.

Sarah turned and fired on the first two. They dropped in a heap on the stairs as the others turned back and took cover.

The mercenaries the team had hired stormed into the kitchen, armed to the teeth.

"Wait! He's our man." Will's voice was a welcome surprise. He patted Vince on the shoulder. "Good to see you, brother. Where is that Russian fuck?"

"Took you long enough to get here! Come on." Vince led the way toward the study.

Sarah looked at the mercs and pointed upstairs. "There are six hostiles upstairs." Then she followed Will and Vince to the study.

She remembered her date with Nikolai in Las Vegas, before her last mission and before she knew he was a ruthless international arms dealer. How charming he'd been. She could be charming to her targets too. She'd charmed Hassan before she killed him, and Victor too. The realization that she and Nikolai worked people over in the very same way hit her right between the eyes. In order to end this, either she or Nikolai had to die.

When they stormed into the study, Nikolai was nowhere to be found. Gunfire rang out upstairs.

Vince and Will searched the room while Sarah watched the door but there was no sign of Nikolai anywhere.

The mercs who had come in from the kitchen rushed through the hallway.

"Any sign of Nikolai?" Anxiety pulled at Sarah's stomach.

"No. We got the guys upstairs but nobody resembling the Russian."

Will remained in charge. "You guys sweep the interior. Don't forget the basement. We've got to get this guy before we go." Will motioned to Vince. "Vince, Sarah, let's get outside and see if they got him out there."

Sarah, Vince, and Will strode out the front door.

The Blackhawk helicopter purred as it circled overhead.

Will glanced up. "Eye in the sky, you see anybody get out?" He paused as Jason responded.

"Just the old lady. Nobody else within two clicks, chief."

"All right, bring it down. It's all clear."

Will looked at Vince and Sarah. "Are there any tunnels?"

Sarah shook her head. "I never saw any, Will."

One of the mercs summoned Will from the house. "Hey, Chief! We got somebody here."

Sarah looked at the doorway and her heart sank when she saw who walked through it.

Samara?

"Fuck!" It was the first time Sarah had seen Will lose his composure through all of this.

"Oh, God. He got away in her abaya." Sarah ran to Samara. "Are you all right? Did he hurt you?"

"He held a gun to me but I am fine. I am so sorry, Sarah."

Brian ran up to Samara. "Did he harm you?"

She shook her head as tears streamed down her cheeks.

Brian looked over toward Will. "We've got Vince, but Nikolai is a bust. I'm gonna get Samara a truck and send her home. She needs to get the hell out of here before the Saudi Air Force shows up."

As if on cue, Jason's voice came through their earpieces. "We've got low flyers, two of them, six minutes out."

Will gave the sign to rally. "The Saudis are on the way! Move it out guys. Let's go!"

The mercs scrambled for the trucks and chopper according to the extraction plan Will had laid out for them.

When Brian's truck wouldn't start, he and his crew jumped in one of the SUVs in the yard and hotwired it. The truck and SUV, both loaded with men, kicked up a trail of dust as they tore out of the compound.

"Okay, boys. Want to see something special?" Jason, hovering above the scene in the Blackhawk, didn't wait for an answer. He launched four hellfire missiles at the house and everything left in the compound was decimated.

Sarah watched the smoke rise as they flew off at nearly two hundred miles per hour. She realized that leaving in the wake of an explosion, or at least a gunfight, was becoming a pattern in her life. Her first mission ended with a multi-million dollar yacht exploding. The second left a bullet riddled, blood stained mansion on the coast of Italy, and now a mansion reduced to smoke and dust.

The helicopter arrived back at the Bedouin camp in minutes. The tents had been taken down and moved out by Brian's cousins. Chris waited by the civilian chopper with his two merc bodyguards. Jason kept the Blackhawk running while Chris threw his bag in and jumped into a seat.

Brian pulled up in a cloud of dust along with another truck full of the contractors. All of the hired men dropped their weapons in the back of the truck and scrambled into the civilian chopper that Brian was powering up.

Sarah hadn't seen him at the compound but Hamza was there. He hopped into the truck loaded with guns and drove like a bat out of hell toward the remote cave that would hide the truck and equipment from the Saudis until the heat was off.

They hadn't had any casualties, and Sarah crossed her fingers, hoping that they'd get both choppers out of Saudi airspace before they were spotted.

Jason's voice came through again on Sarah's earpiece. "The Saudi's have Blackhawks too, so let's light a fire, kids."

Both choppers lifted off from the campsite.

Brian flew the civilian chopper, loaded with well-paid mercenaries northeast, toward the cities, while Jason flew the Blackhawk carrying Guinea, Vince, Sarah, Will, and Chris southeast toward an empty corridor so they could fly back to the island without being seen. The air and sand blown by the low flying Blackhawk removed every trace of the tracks left by Hamza's truck. He'd sleep in the cave until morning and then drive home in the truck loaded with guns, a bonus for his assistance.

Thirty-Three

The morning after Vince's rescue was almost like any other off-duty morning at Brian's house in Las Vegas, only they were on Vince's island off the coast of Dubai. Sarah crept into the empty kitchen. She'd gathered from the quiet house that she was the first one awake. She brewed the first pot of coffee and poured herself a cup, anxious to start her caffeine infusion. She took a quick sip and cursed as she burned the tip of her tongue. With Vince back, she had plans for that tongue. She closed her eyes and shivered at the delicious thought of making love to Vince again.

She stood in silent bliss after her first good night's sleep in over a week, reflecting on how well Will had handled the arrangements for the mercenaries they'd hired. If all went as planned, the men had been flown directly to the airport in Dubai after the operation and ushered onto a chartered jet. They would be flown directly to a small municipal airport in North Carolina and transported immediately to Sentrion headquarters where Brock Benjamin would debrief them. Knowing how agents and ex agents worked, Sarah assumed Brock would file the information in a special safe deposit box kept specifically for recording the details of secret contracts he'd either take to his grave or use to call in favors later.

Sarah had slept easy the night before knowing Vince and their teammates were safe, though a tiny whisper at the back of her mind told her Nikolai was still out there and more dangerous than ever.

Jason strolled into the kitchen wearing a tan T-shirt and brown canvas cargo shorts. The smile on his face told Sarah his night of destruction in the Blackhawk had been nearly as satisfying as getting laid, only without the awkward morning after. "So we're meeting a spook with an official cover at his beach house in Dubai? Doesn't this smell funny to anyone?"

Sarah poured and Jason drank. It was a rhetorical question and she knew it. Mark Davidson had done them a huge favor and now wanted to see all of them at his beach house for a barbeque. It seemed too simple.

Will chose that moment to appear and poured himself a cup. "Jason, do I have to remind you the man gave us the information we needed to pull Vince out of a very bad situation?"

Vince ambled into the kitchen, battered but not broken. He grabbed a huge coffee cup with a gold U.S. Marines seal from the back of the cupboard. "Yeah, and I for one would like to know why."

Sarah filled it with coffee as he kissed her on the cheek. She set the pot back on the hotplate. "How are you feeling?"

Vince set his cup on the counter, grinned, and wrapped his arms around her from behind. "Rested."

"How's the rib?"

"Tender but no real damage done." He nuzzled her neck and kissed her earlobe before picking up his coffee.

Relief washed over her, and she smiled as she thought about doing much more than just sleeping in Vince's bed again. "Good."

Chris strolled in from outside through the back door off the kitchen. "I should have known you'd all be standing around the coffee pot."

Vince let go of Sarah and picked up his coffee. "Good morning, Chris. Make sure you pack your bug sweeping gear today. Gratitude doesn't require trust."

"I just put it in the boat." He wrinkled his eyebrows at Vince. "Don't you ever take a day off?"

"Soon." He wrapped an arm around Sarah's waist and pulled her close.

Brian strolled into the kitchen shaking his head. "Twenty-nine foot Rockit speedboat. Not a bad way to get around the coast, man." There was mischief in his eyes when he smiled at Vince. "When we're finished with Davidson, I'd like to take that baby out and open her up."

Vince took a long gulp of his coffee. "What's mine is yours."

Brian winked at Sarah. "That's good to know." He made his way to the cupboard, retrieved a coffee cup, and then stopped to examine the bruises on Vince's face. "Well, it's a damned good thing you're a spook, brother, because the camera would not like you today."

Vince turned his black eye toward Brian. "You don't like it? The purple is on its way out. I think the green is coming in later today."

Brian poured himself a cup of coffee. "You look much better in monochrome."

Vince flashed a mischievous grin at Brian. "Oh, so you've been noticing how I look, have you?"

"Don't get any ideas. You ain't lookin' good. You've lost a lot of muscle. You look flat. The only good thing being drugged unconscious and not eating for a few days did for you was cut the extra body fat you put on eating all that pasta in Italy. You need to get back to heavy protein and good supplements if you want your muscle back."

"Yeah, I know."

Jason set his cup down. "Okay, girls, enough beauty talk. Are we ready to get going?"

Vince gulped his coffee in one chug. "Yeah, let's go find out what this guy's game is."

~~~

"Oh, man! It is great to see you!" Davidson seemed genuinely happy to see Vince. He shook his hand and then looked at Vince's face. "If it weren't for the black eye, I'd never be able to tell the difference between you and Rig."

Vince chuckled. "So that's it. You know my brother?"

"Rigatoni Hennessee! Biggest pain in the ass I ever met. Let's get out of view." Davidson motioned for everyone to follow him up the dock.

Sarah whispered to Vince. "Rigatoni? Your parents named your brother after pasta?"

"No." Vince laughed. "His name is Anthony and our parents called him Tony, but we used to call him Rigatoni when we wanted to tick him off. The name stuck, and we shortened it to Rig when we got older. That's what he goes by now."

Davidson ushered them into a magnificent coral-colored, stucco beach house.

Buffy greeted them in a miniscule sundress that showed off her more than ample cleavage.

Introductions were made and Buffy insisted they all make themselves comfortable.

Vince shot Chris a glance and a nod.

Chris opened a small minicomputer, tapped a few buttons and within seconds he gave Vince the *'all clear.'*

Davidson took it in stride. "We had the house swept yesterday. Bugging is an occupational hazard in the State Department." He led them into a large, sunny living room. "Come on in and have a seat." Overstuffed chairs and sofas were arranged around a large, low coffee table.

The furniture and the carpet were the same cream-colored beige. The only non-neutral color in the room was the foliage. Tropical flowers and plants were tastefully placed around the room. Large potted palm trees stood in the corners of the room like sentinels. Sarah could hear calypso music coming from everywhere but never saw a single speaker.

Davidson retrieved a small humidor from a shelf and offered cigars as everyone sat in the cloudlike chairs. "I can't think of a better reason to smoke a cigar."

Will and Vince each took a cigar.

Sarah lit a cigarette while they trimmed and lit their cigars.

Buffy flashed a brilliant smile. "What would everyone like to drink? I have margaritas by the pitcher and a full bar."

Davidson returned the humidor to its shelf and walked over to the large bar in the corner. "Vince, I'm guessing you like a nice Scotch with a cigar?"

"That would be great."

Davidson gave his wife a playful pat on the ass before pouring the Scotch. "Anyone else?"

Will perked up. "I'll have some of that, Mark. The Scotch, that is."

Buffy blushed slightly as she carried a crystal pitcher of margaritas, a crystal ice bucket, and several glasses on a silver tray and set it down on the coffee table. Brian, Jason, Sarah, and Chris helped themselves.

Once they'd all settled in with their cigars and drinks, Vince spoke. "Mark, I want to thank you for your help. You know the Agency's policy on this sort of thing, and you took a real risk helping us out. I owe you for that."

"You don't owe me anything. I'm just trying to pay back an old debt."

Vince shook his head. "I don't understand."

"Then I'm going to tell you a story." He sat back in his chair. "Way back in the day, your brother Rig and I were a couple of enlisted troops who both happened to land in Saudi Arabia on the very same day. He was hot for a lifting buddy to go work out with him and set his sights on me because we were both about the same build. I'd never lifted a weight in my life if I could help it." He took a sip of his Scotch. "I hated the idea of working out and told him so. He wouldn't take no for an answer and kept knocking on my door every day before our shift. I kept blowing him off. I must have told him to go to hell every day for two weeks straight before he finally wore me down." Davidson shook his head. "He's a persistent bastard."

Vince nodded in agreement. "That he is."

"So the day of our first workout, Rig and I were in the base gym when somebody parked a car bomb by the base fence. We heard the explosion and ran back to the barracks from the gym. When we got there, my room was gone." Mark took a deep breath and exhaled slowly. "I mean there was no sign of it. The Khobar Towers had been blown to shit. If I had slept just a little later, I'd have been a stain on concrete rubble."

"Jesus." Jason lit a cigarette.

Davidson smiled and nodded. "I haven't missed a workout since. Every time I walk into a gym, I remember that I owe that persistent, pasta-eating fucker my life." He motioned to Vince. "No disrespect."

Vince shook his head. "None taken. He is a fucker, and he is persistent."

"So when I got the news about Vince, I had to do something. Helping you get out of the clutches of the Red Menace was my way of paying back a little. I'm just glad you guys knew how to put together a team and make it happen because my tactical knowledge is confined to military working dogs."

Will chuckled.

Davidson raised an eyebrow at Will. "So did you manage to get all your houseguests off without any hassles?" He took a puff of his cigar, rolled it between his thumb and forefinger, and smiled at Will while he waited for an answer.

Will mimicked Davidson's mannerisms and smiled. "I don't know what you're talking about. We never had houseguests."

Something was understood among everyone in the room, and Sarah didn't miss it either. Davidson was smart, loyal, had great intelligence connections, and was the kind of guy you wanted on your side in a fight.

He wasn't all about the Agency. He had the balls to take care of his friends and that was something they could all respect.

Sarah had assumed Mark had been a career spy, but his last comment raised a question. She spoke up. "Mark, were you a dog handler too?" She looked from Mark to Buffy.

"Yeah, twelve years." He smiled up at Buffy who was perched on the arm of his chair. "I cross-trained and spent my last eight years in the Air Force in intelligence and then got a cushy office with the State Department."

Buffy smiled and rubbed her husband's back. "Not a bad career path."

Davidson set his empty glass on the table and rested his cigar on the ashtray. "Now who wants ribs and who wants burgers?"

Thirty-Four

A warm, happy feeling filled Sarah as she hung up the phone and made her way through the living room.

Jason, Chris, Guinea, and Brian would be distracted for quite some time with the video game they were playing.

She walked upstairs to the gym and found Vince there, shirtless and sweating from his usual heavy workout.

She leaned against the doorway. "We did it. Samara and Bashira arrived safely at the villa in Italy. They seem very happy with their cottage and start studying with their language tutor tomorrow."

Vince finished his lift and racked the bar. "Nice work, babe. You did a good thing."

"Bashira needed a new start someplace where being a victim isn't a crime." Sarah took a deep breath and wished she could do more to help women like Bashira. She had to be satisfied with the little bit she could do.

Vince looked up from the bench he was lying on. "This isn't a peep show, girl. You plan to exercise?"

Sarah woke from her thoughts and walked over to Vince. She straddled him on the bench. "Hell, yeah, I plan to exercise. How do feel about some horizontal aerobics?"

"Mmm." Vince growled and pulled himself upright, wrapping his arms around Sarah. "There ain't nothing horizontal in this room but this bench."

The sound of his growl set off a warmth and need between her legs. Desire overwhelmed her as her body responded to the hard length she was sitting on. "It is so good to have you back." She ran her hands over Vince's shoulders and eased her hips forward. She closed her eyes as a groan escaped her lips. "Do we have time?"

"Baby, we always have time."

Enjoy A Sneak Peek Of Stealing Liberties, Book 4

in the Task Force 125 Series

Moscow

Konstantin folded the dead man's lifeless limbs around the still warm torso and tucked the corpse into the large plastic garment bag before zipping the makeshift body-bag closed. He hefted the awkward package over his shoulder and dropped it into the trunk of his BMW with a *thunk*. He slammed the trunk closed and walked around the sedan to climb into the driver's seat.

His phone chirped.

Konstantin pressed the button on the steering wheel to answer as he started the car. "Da."

"I have a cleaning job for you."

Konstantin recognized Nikolai Federov's voice. "Good. I just finished the last one." Nikolai's childish grudges over social slights had been keeping Konstantin busy with hits for the past several weeks, but who was Konstantin to judge? Nikolai's ultra-sensitive, paranoid personality, mixed with his deep pockets were about to finance Konstantin's early retirement.

"This one has three parts, all foreign, all highly skilled, and there's a bonus."

Konstantin considered the possibilities. Foreign hits were more difficult because they involved acquiring weapons after traveling into a foreign country. Travel itself posed a challenge as he was barred from several countries already. A highly skilled target was one he couldn't pass up though. Most of his hits had been ducks in a barrel. Boredom had set in lately and a challenge could bring back the spark. A target with skills would be a pleasure. He grinned as he drove off the gravel road and onto the highway. "Ahh…I love a good challenge."

"Come to my office for the details."

"I'll be there."

Las Vegas

Vince Hennessee lay in bed, unable to sleep, staring at the ceiling and listening to Sarah's soft breathing. She'd gone to sleep soon after they'd made love. She'd probably sleep for quite some time. Sarah Stevens was the kind of woman he'd always wanted. She was strong and capable one minute, and soft and loving the next. She was a mix of exquisite contradictions. She had the world by the balls and she was beginning to know it. Any man would be a fool to let her slip away, and Antonia Hennessee didn't raise any fools. The only problem was timing. He'd done something against his better judgment after Sarah and the team rescued him from Nikolai's compound. He'd spent a magical week alone with Sarah on the island he'd bought with gun money, courtesy of, but unbeknownst to the U.S. government. The lure of an idyllic life together had been too much. He'd presented her with a four-carat diamond and asked her to marry him even though he knew their timing was all wrong and they'd have to set aside their love affair to get back to the work of being Paramilitary Operations Officers with the Central Intelligence Agency. He gave a short chuckle at the title. They were spies who specialized in wet-work, assassinations, for "the agency". Relationships didn't always pan out for clandestine agents working undercover, and life as a Force Recon Marine had never been conducive to a happy home life, but Vince reveled in the dream of domestic bliss with the right woman. Being here with someone like Sarah was what he wanted, all he'd ever wanted.

He rested his arm on his forehead. *Is it too much to ask for just a simple, uncomplicated life?*

Nikolai Federov, the Russian mob captain they'd failed to liquidate during their last mission who had subsequently succeeded in kidnapping Vince, was still at large, and that meant Federov still had guys watching Sarah. She and Vince might have everything they needed, but a simple, happy life would always be tenuous at best until they found Nikolai and buried him. Thanks to a very generous, and now deceased, ex lover, Sarah had all the money she'd ever need to assume an alias, so she'd just given the CIA their walking papers and told the Agency she was leaving the business. Guilt tore at Vince. Nikolai's life had to end if theirs was to begin, and it wasn't right to let Sarah believe they had a chance at making a future together yet.

Maybe we can get Nikolai quickly and then run away together?

The cell phone on the bedside table rang and interrupted his dark thoughts. He snatched it up and quickly checked the time. The screen said five AM. He rolled his eyes and tried to keep his voice low. "Hennessee."

Sarah reached over, her eyes still closed, and laid a soft, warm hand on his shoulder.

Vince turned his head toward the touch and gently kissed a newly manicured fingertip.

"It's Philippo. If anyone asks, I didn't tell you but there's a contract out on you."

Vince's stomach tumbled. He'd played spy games with the world's worst bad guys for years but this was the first contract put on him. If Philippo felt it was worth calling about then the reward offered had to be a big one. Vince gently moved Sarah's hand onto his pillow and slid off the bed. He held the phone between his chin and shoulder as he slipped on a pair of Jeans. He'd been expecting this after Federov escaped when the team rescued him and destroyed Federov's compound in Saudi Arabia. What he really needed to know was how big the price tag was so he'd know what kind of contract killers to expect. "How much?" He plodded barefoot into Sarah's kitchen to make some coffee.

"Three hundred thousand dollars each for you, Will Adams, and Sarah Stevens. An extra hundred thousand bonus has been offered for anyone who can take down all three of you."

This is serious shit.

Vince grunted. "Not a bad price."

Not a good situation. A Russian'll do a street hit anywhere in the country for a grand. This kind of money would bring out the big players, the Ukrainian hit men that would track their targets around the world like dogs, stuff them in a box and ship them first class to the client who posted the contract.

He pushed the button to start the already prepared coffee maker.

Gotta love that girl's nightly routine.

"A million for the whole set, huh?"

"I'm afraid so, my friend."

Vince bit his lip and considered which hit men he knew who would likely take the challenge. A few good ones came to mind. "Any takers on the contract yet?"

The coffee maker gurgled and his stomach growled.

"A few up-and-comers, mostly Ukrainians. You know how they love big game."

"Thanks, Phil."

"Good luck."

Vince clicked off and set his cell phone on the kitchen counter.

This kind of contract could make a man's career a legend.

He poured two cups of coffee and his phone rang again.

"Vince. It's Mark Davidson."

"Hey, Mark. How are you?" Vince drank from his cup, grateful for the warm liquid that would power him through what was shaping up to be a hard day.

"I'm doing well, thanks. Listen, this isn't really a social call. I wanted to let you know I've received an assignment transfer."

"Oh, yeah? Where to?"

"Buffy and I thought it would be nice to see Moscow. She's crazy for shopping and the furs are ridiculous."

Vince smiled. "Buffy's a spitfire, but give me a happy housewife any day. You're a good man to plan around your wife's shopping needs."

"Yeah, so she tells me."

"Are you there now?" Vince rubbed the back of his neck. Davidson was a power player in the CIA. This phone call had to be important.

" We just moved in and I've had a few days at the office. You'll never guess who I heard was in town."

"Hmm…" Vince took another drink of coffee and set his cup back on the counter. "An old, not so friendly friend of mine named Nikolai, maybe?"

"That's right. Seems he's come back to the bosom of the motherland to feel the love, so to speak."

"That's good to know, Mark." Vince rubbed his eyes with his free hand. A dull ache throbbed in the center of his forehead.

"I don't know what your plans are, but if you decide to come out for a visit, I could make some arrangements for you, put you in touch with some people who might help you out."

"As a matter of fact, I was just getting my travel plans together for a little trip out that way."

"Excellent. Let me talk to a friend of mine and I'll email you some information later today. Do you have a flight yet?"

"I'll leave tomorrow."

Sarah won't be happy, but she understands the nature of the spy business and will eventually understand. The sooner we get this done, the sooner we can get married, have a half dozen kids and a happy life in Idaho.

"Good. Word has it Nikolai is working on some projects that may be of interest to both of us. The sooner you pay a visit the better."

You mean the sooner I kill him, the better. CIA desk jockeys were all the same. They all wanted to put hits out on new targets, but while the field agents like Vince were getting blood on their hands, guys like Davidson were buying their wives minks or new boobs.

"I'll be waiting for that email. Thanks for the call, Mark."

"No problem, Vince. Stay safe."

Vince clicked off, slipped the phone into his pocket and grabbed both coffee mugs before walking back into Sarah's bedroom.

~~~

Sarah watched Vince walk into the room looking like he carried the weight of the world. An icy trickle of apprehension flowed down her spine. "What is it?"

Vince walked over to her side of the bed and smiled as Sarah sat up. He handed her a cup of coffee as he sat on the edge of the bed and took a sip of his own. "A friend of mine in the contracts business just called. Nikolai's got contracts out on us."

Sarah nodded. "We expected that." She put her coffee cup on the bedside table and tried to reassure him with a gentle hand on his shoulder. "We've got aliases and enough money to go anywhere. He'll never find us."

"We can't run. He's offered a high price." He shook his head. "I should have known we couldn't pull this off yet."

She snuggled against his shoulder and ran her hand along his thigh. Confusion hit Sarah as she saw an unsure Vince for the very first time. "We can do this together. We've got the resources and the connections we need to quit this life and start one together. Let the next agents in line take on Nikolai."

"You know we'll never be safe until we find him. It'll always be him or us." He looked down at his knees. "We can do this, but we'll be sitting ducks if we try to do it together."

"Why? We're a good team." Her gut told her he'd already made a decision and this wasn't going to be a discussion but a notification. She wasn't ready to accept what she suspected he was about to do. "Vince, we can do this!"

"Don't you see, Sarah? When Nikolai kidnapped me, the Agency wrote me off. As far as they're concerned I'm missing in action. I can go anywhere now."

"Yes, and so can I. My contract with the Agency has been cleared. They accepted my resignation." Sarah's stomach knotted. She rubbed her eyes and wondered how she could convince Vince not to do this on his own. He seemed too unsure of himself to handle it, and she wondered why she'd never seen this side of him before. "What are you trying to tell me, Vince?"

Vince stood and took a deep breath before he spoke. He turned to face her. "If you take one more assignment with the team, we'll have a chance to draw Nikolai out. He wanted us before, but he's hot for our heads now that he's seen his house leveled to rubble and dust."

He hates the idea of me working for the Agency. He's mentioned it a hundred times in the past three weeks. Why his sudden weakness and indecisiveness?

Sarah jumped up and stood toe to toe with Vince. "What the hell? No way!" Sarah turned and paced a few steps before turning back to glare at Vince. "I've already resigned my position with the agency. They've closed my file and I have a new identity."

"Don't you see?" He seemed earnest. "If you take another assignment and leave your party girl trail, he'll be all over you."

Is this some kind of fucked up loyalty test to see if I'll take the bait? He knows I loved that job but I gave it up because he wanted me to.

"Let me get this straight." She held her fist up and raised a finger to make each successive point. "I have a villa in Italy with a profitable vineyard, a condo in Las Vegas, and more money than God, but instead of just running away together to live the good life, you want me to take another assignment and go fuck some bad boy on the CIA's most wanted list?" In all the assignments she'd taken, she'd had to play the Honey Pot, the sex kitten they dropped in to bait the target. This was the first time she'd ever felt like someone was pimping her out, and it was Vince doing it. She raised her voice now but she didn't give a damn. What he was suggesting was cowardly, foolhardy and stupid when an easy out stared them in the face. "You want me to leave a trail so you can get a second shot at Nikolai when the first one went so well?"

He flinched and stared at her, wide-eyed.

The last comment was meant to hurt him. Nikolai had been a step ahead of Vince when he'd left Italy to assassinate Federov. Nikolai had Vince kidnapped instead. If Sarah and the rest of the team hadn't pooled their resources, broken a lot of international laws, and had some damned good luck, Vince would be in a shallow grave somewhere in Saudi Arabia right now. She rubbed her forehead. "Who are you? And what have you done with Vince Hennessee?"

"No, baby." Vince reached out to her but she deflected his grasp and glared at him instead. "No. I'm talking about being able to protect you. If you're the bait, I can circle around and get him before he takes his shot at you."

Fuck that. Your skills have been slipping.

Her faith in his abilities was waning fast, and this last attempt of his hadn't helped. Her stomach turned as she realized she couldn't trust him. She shrugged him off and continued pacing. "No, I don't like it. There's too much risk. I don't like it at all." She balled her fists at her side and eyed him. She hated that she couldn't trust him to have her back and make a simple hit. But she had to follow her gut. "While you're out there, who'll have your back? You'll be on your own with no support at all. What if something happens to you again?"

Because it will.

Sarah bent to pick up a T-shirt he'd left lying on the floor. "I don't want to go through that again." She threw the T-shirt into the laundry basket in the corner and continued pacing. She softened her tone, hoping to appeal to Vince's feelings for her. "Do you have any idea how hard it was for me to just stand there while Nikolai's goons tied you to a chair and beat you to a bloody pulp?" Her voice cracked and she hated herself for the weakness it showed. "Do you have any idea what that did to me?" He'd walked himself into a trap and she'd had to witness his torture firsthand. It had torn at her heart then as it did now, but fear had given way to pity.

He's lost his edge.

Vince grabbed Sarah by the shoulders and fixed her with his soft brown gaze. "And do you have any idea what it would do to me if Nikolai got *you*? He'd do much more than slap you around and break a few ribs. Sarah, they'd do the worst things a man can do to a woman. You would die a slow, painful, gruesome death."

She shuddered. She'd heard the rape and torture stories. There was a special briefing just for women who joined the clandestine service to prepare them for what could happen if they were captured.

He trailed his fingers gently down her arms to hold her hands. "You've got to understand. I've been doing this sort of thing for a long time. I know how these people think. We can make this plan work so nobody but Nikolai will get hurt."

You aren't the man I thought you were. You've let your emotions take control of that once analytical mind. Running off half-cocked to save me is not a strategy.

Sarah's heart ached. She used to think she wanted to settle down with a guy like Vince and live happily ever after, but how would she find happily ever after knowing he could be so weak and unsure of himself? Flashbacks from the past year played out at hyperspeed inside her mind. Vince had taken a taxi to a commercial airport and got kidnapped before he even made it past security. That wasn't the work of a seasoned spy. The job in Italy went to shit and they lost good men. Even Sarah had taken a bullet.

He'[d grown sloppy. After only two years in the agency, and she knew it. What was his excuse after years in the Marines and just as many years as an arms dealer for the agency? Her assumptions and the dreams of her past slipped away. No, this was not the future she wanted. She shook free of his grasp, took a deep breath and a stepped back. "No." She shook her head. "There has to be another way."

Vince grabbed Sarah around the waist and pulled her close.

She turned to look away.

"What do you think I've been doing for the past week? I lie awake at night trying to work out how we can get our happily ever after. I've worked through every scenario a hundred times in my head. The only thing that makes sense is for us to bait and flank him. It's the only way."

Sarah sighed and looked at a once great man now grasping at straws. Her voice softened and she touched his cheek. "Wake up Vince. We aren't going to get that happily ever after."

"We still can. We can still have it all, Sarah. Just not yet. One more job and we can do it."

We need to face the truth. We're targets for too many terrorists. Everybody wants us dead.

Sarah hugged Vince, holding on to him as dreams from a past life washed away like sand under the tide. This morning her life had changed completely. Or maybe it had been changing over the past two years and she was only now seeing what it had become? Her head and her gut told her that tactically, baiting Nikolai and assassinating him was the right move, but having Vince out there alone to take the shot after he'd lost his edge was wrong. He needed the whole team to make it work.

We might get Nikolai but we'll never be together.

She hadn't wanted to fall in love again. She'd had no intention of doing so. This morning, she'd realized she'd fallen out.

He must know it too.

Her heart ached.

"I've spoken to Mark Davidson. He's been transferred to Moscow and has some people keeping an eye on Nikolai."

Sarah broke from Vince's grasp and walked to the sliding glass door that led out to the patio of her luxury condo at The Signature at MGM Grand.

The sun was coming up in Las Vegas and the staff was arranging the chairs by the pool far below.

Mark is a player, not a killer. Vince needs real men behind him on this operation.

"If Mark has people on him why can't he just make Nikolai disappear? Why can't we hire a gun to do it for us?"

Vince inhaled hard through his teeth. "You know it doesn't work like that. Mark has an official cover with his state department job. If he uses that job to go out and exterminate some Russian, he's looking at prison time, quite possibly in Russia. Do you have any idea what the Russian prison system is like?"

Her cheeks burned and she blinked hard to hide the angry tears that had formed.

I never cry. I never fucking cry except when I'm mad as hell and then it just looks weak.

She lowered her voice to a growl. "How many languages do I speak? How many dead men have underestimated me, just like you're doing now? Do you mean to tell me you still think I'm just another pretty face? After two years of operations and me putting my life on the line for you more than once, you still think I'm just a frail, dumb woman?" She swallowed the ball of bile she wanted to spit at Vince and ran a hand through her hair. "Screw you. Don't let my cover confuse you as to who I really am." She spun around to shoot lightning bolts at the wall so she wouldn't punch him in the face.

His breath was slow and loud behind her. "Look, we can do this ourselves. Davidson has some connections I can use. The team has a mission brief the day after tomorrow so I'll leave for Moscow tomorrow."

And you'll die there unless you suddenly pull a guardian angel out of your ass.

Sarah turned to see him sitting on the edge of the bed, shoulders slumped. The magic they'd shared together had been sucked out of the room. She didn't know the man sitting on her bed.

They'd only had a couple weeks together. It had been like a honeymoon, the two of them on their own island, making love, swimming, lying around with no worries and nobody to bother them. It had been idyllic. Now they were back in Las Vegas and the only mirage left was the hotel on the strip.

Vince's phone rang, and she watched as he pulled it from his pocket.

"It's Davidson." He never hesitated to answer it.

Reality hit. It was over. He had no intention of ever discussing any of this with her to get her input. His plan was to throw her out there as bait. Chum for the sharks.

Well, fuck you.

She walked into the kitchen and placed a call of her own.

"Full name please?"

"Sarah Marie Stevens."

"How may I direct your call?"

"Young."

Sarah waited while the operator at The Camp connected her to the man who was her team's handler. The man who had just recently accepted her resignation. Their team, American Swift, was like every other paramilitary team in The Agency's arsenal. They had a 'handler'. Colonel Young was a monster of a man with a chest the size of Mount McKinley and biceps to match. Sarah suspected he was at least part Samoan but never bothered to ask as he was never one to encourage chit-chat. For good reason too. Colonel Young worked in that black world where the U.S. military and her spies mixed to create the most deadly personnel possible, those with intelligent, analytical minds and a patriotic streak so wide they could look at a human being, see a target and eliminate it without remorse. "Wetwork" was the impersonal, industry term for American Swift's line of work.

"Hey, Sarah, how's retired life?"

"Put me back in."

"I knew you'd be back. See you tomorrow."

What was the world coming to when a prick like Young knew her better than her fiancé did? She paused a moment as she realized spy work was her element but love scared the hell out of her.

Maybe I have more in common with the pricks than the heroes now? Maybe the pricks are the real heroes? I don't really care anymore.

About The Author

Lisa Pietsch (pen name of Lisa Woodward) is the Publishing Director at Defiance Press and Publishing, an Air Force Veteran, former magazine publisher, multi-published author, mother of two giants, and wife to a Viking.

Lisa speaks French, Spanish, Norwegian, and Russian. She has been USAF Security Forces Leader, received specialized training as an FBI Hostage Negotiator, and worked with MI-5 on personal security details for both British and Jordanian Royals. These diverse experiences inspire her Task Force 125 series, which follows Sarah Stevens, a CIA Special Activities Division recruit, through gripping tales of espionage and paramilitary operations.

In 2020, Lisa's life took a romantic turn when she reconnected with the love of her life, the man who inspired her Task Force 125 series, launching her into her greatest adventure yet.

An avid gamer, Lisa enjoys both console and tabletop gaming, where she goes by "Geniekin" on Xbox and Roll20.

As Lisa Pietsch, she crafts thrilling paramilitary action/adventure/romance novels, while as Lisa Woodward, she weaves enchanting epic romantic fantasy tales.

www.ingramcontent.com/pod-product-compliance
Lightning Source LLC
Chambersburg PA
CBHW051110030726
47504CB00006B/1873